Every Witch Way but Lost

Magical Misfits Mysteries - book 18

K.E. O'Connor

K.E. O'Connor Books

Chapter 1

Tricky times

"You sneak around the other side and get in front, while I cause a distraction. Then you grab them. Do you have your protective gloves?" I focused on the gaggle of fast-moving, troublesome, not to mention gassy, enchanted hedgehogs.

"I've got them in my back pocket," Zandra Crypt, my most wonderful witchy sidekick, whispered.

We'd been chasing these prickly customers for days, and they proved to be our most elusive and difficult capture in weeks. And we'd had plenty of practice tackling difficult, recently.

Zandra and I had worked double shifts most days to keep on top of the crazy workload being shoved through animal control. And it wasn't because of a lack of staff, since everyone had been pulled in. We were tackling as many jobs as we could.

But it wasn't enough. Every morning, residents were outside the door ready to complain about an out-of-control toad or angry hound causing havoc in Crimson Cove.

Our boss, Barney Hoffman, spent his days sending messages to get more resources, fielding calls, handling angry residents, or looking at the budget with haggard eyes to find money for temporary staff.

There had been times in the past when Crimson Cove's enchanted creatures strained our schedule, but it hadn't been like this for a long time. It was one of the many examples that all was far from well in Crimson Cove.

"Look out for their shooting prickles," I hiss-whispered.

Zandra crept away on her tiptoes, magic sparking on her fingertips. "I will. I haven't forgotten our first encounter with enchanted hedgehogs."

"Neither have I. I sucked the quill poison from your cheek," I whispered. "Just don't get distracted, and you'll be fine."

Zandra absently rubbed her cheek where there were still tiny red marks where the quills had embedded deeply.

Enchanted hedgehogs shouldn't be a difficult capture. After all, they were small, not usually fast, and although their quills were unpleasant when embedded into your flesh, they had no deadly weapons.

But there was something different about these hedgehogs. It was as if they'd had a power boost. All capture attempts had failed, and they moved so swiftly that they had to be getting a magic injection of something special from somewhere.

This wasn't the only strange magic floating around Crimson Cove and causing trouble.

Oddness had been going on for months, and it was getting worse by the day.

I made a show of stalking the hedgehogs, hissing and swiping out a murder mitten to keep their interest on me. It caused them to squeak and fling out poisonous quills in a haphazard, scattered pattern.

I hissed and danced in front of the hedgehogs, hoping to confuse them and herd them toward Zandra.

Rather than fleeing in terror at the sight of my mighty strength and fleet of paw movements, they laughed.

Pesky little critters. We'd make them sorry for wasting so much of our time. They'd been menacing this town, and we had enough jobs on our paws.

I checked where Zandra was and glimpsed the top of her head as she crouched behind a bush close to the hedgehogs.

She peeked over the top of the bush and nodded to let me know she was ready to fix this prickly problem once and for all.

I bounced about on my paws and sparked magic at the hedgehogs, but something felt wrong with the spell. Instead of floating around me in a showy display, it whipped away from my paw and slammed into an ancient tree trunk, splintering the wood and causing a fracture to the base. The damage grew, spreading up the entire length of the trunk.

The tree creaked ominously, causing the hedgehogs to squeak in genuine alarm, and a few seconds later, the entire tree was crashing toward us.

I thrust out a counterspell to lessen the impact, shocked my magic had such an effect.

The spell encircled the falling tree, lifted it, and smashed it into the ground, knocking me off my paws.

"Juno! Are you hurt?" Zandra leaped over the tree and raced toward me, all thoughts of the enchanted hedgehog capture gone.

"Not hurt. Just shocked." I dusted myself down with a vigorous shake and stared at the fallen tree.

"I know you wanted to cause a distraction, but that was extreme." Zandra flipped her dark hair out of her eyes as she stared at the fallen tree. "You'll have the town's forest guardian after you for that."

"I didn't mean to do it!" I stared at the sad, fallen giant. That tree had probably been standing for hundreds of years, and my wonky spell destroyed it. I blamed the hedgehogs.

Zandra tilted her head. "You've been saying that a lot lately."

"Sometimes, even someone as perfect as me is off their game. Look out!" I shoved Zandra by bouncing on her chest just as a barrage of quills flew through the air, aimed at her head.

We tumbled to the ground, and I shielded us with a protection spell in case the hedgehogs struck while we were down.

I peered out from underneath Zandra. "Those hedgehogs did something to my spell to make it backfire and kill the tree."

"We can worry about who to blame later. We need to stop them!" Zandra scrambled to her feet, crouched, ready to run and bring down the troublesome hoggies for good.

I rolled to my paws, shaking leaves out of my glorious white fur. A scan of the area showed no hedgehogs about to pounce. I couldn't even smell their distinctive gaseous stink that grew even more pungent as their fear heightened.

"They've escaped!" Zandra peered around the forest in Crimson Cove, where we'd been tracking the hedgehogs for hours. "No! Wait! There they are. We're not letting them get away this time."

Together, we dashed past trees, dodging around bushes, determined to stop those hedgehogs once and for all and end their prickly pestering.

"This is like the good old days," Zandra said with a smile. "Remember our first case?"

"I remember setting traps to capture hedgehogs, and then Torrin destroyed a cage and ate them."

"Which he regretted when they repeated on him like a week-old curry," Zandra said.

"Not even someone who's part dragon can digest enchanted hedgehog quills. They were happy to go into the cages after he burped them up covered in dragon spit."

I leaped over another fallen log. "It's strange they're so riled."

"They're like everyone else," Zandra said. "This town is full of pent-up rage and frustration."

"It's the glitchy magic," I said. "No magic user is happy when their abilities misbehave."

Zandra slid me a curious glance as we continued our pursuit. Strange magic had been a topic we'd been skirting for some time. I'd used less-than-appropriate magic to help her forget I was something special. And when that went wrong, I'd made excuses, so we wouldn't need to talk about it. But I'd run out of excuses, and I could sense the end was near.

When the truth came out, what else would end? Zandra could hold a grudge. She'd resent me for keeping this information from her. How deeply would that resentment go? It would soon be time to find out.

"Hey! Did you see? They went into that tree trunk," Zandra said. "They've trapped themselves."

We stopped outside a hole in an ancient, half-rotten tree. The tree looked almost dead, although a few new leaves fluttered overhead, suggesting it hadn't quite given up the fight.

"Come out," I yelled. "You've got nowhere to go. You have to come into animal control and explain why throwing stink quills at children would ever be acceptable behavior."

There was a shuffling inside the tree trunk, but no hedgehogs appeared.

"We won't hurt you," Zandra said, out of breath from running. "But until you learn to behave and stop misusing your magic, you can't remain free roaming. You've injured several people."

There were indignant hisses from inside the tree trunk.

"There's no point in having a huff," I said. "You know you've done wrong."

A barrage of quills shot out of the hole, which I dodged just in time.

"That's making it worse," I said. "Fighting us will put another black mark against your already tarnished records."

"We could knock them out," Zandra whispered. "I'll toss in a spell and wait for them to fall asleep. We can bag them and take them back to animal control."

"So long as there's a holding pen for them with glass panels so they can't shoot their quills at anyone," I said. "The last time we were in the office, there was barely anywhere to house the new intake."

"Barney said he's clearing the backlog," Zandra said.

"He's been saying that all week! They'll have to make do with a pen outside," I said. "They're hardy, and we'll feed them and keep them warm. They'll want for nothing."

More quills flew out of the hole. The hoggies clearly hated that idea.

"Time to bring in these prickly monsters." Zandra yanked a quill from her jacket sleeve, sparked a spell, and thrust it into the hole.

The ground rumbled, and an enormous explosion of dirt and rubble caused us to stagger back, landing in an undignified heap.

"What spell did you use?" I blinked dirt out of my eyes.

"A simple knockout spell." Zandra looked down at her fingers and flexed them. "The second I cast, it felt wrong. My magic keeps going wrong."

"You did something right," I said, nodding toward the tree trunk.

The three hedgehogs had rolled out, curled into tight, prickly balls. One of them loudly broke wind.

"Do you think they're safe to approach?" Zandra asked. "They could be faking being asleep to trick us."

"I'll check." I crept toward the hedgehogs, slow and low on my belly. They didn't stir, but I could see they were breathing deeply. "You may have added extra spice to your spell, but they're asleep. It worked."

Zandra was already pulling open a thickly insulated bag that sparkled with a magical containment spell. She yanked on gloves, grabbed each hedgehog, and tucked them into the bag. "Success at last."

"That deserves a sit-down and a treat. I'm in the mood for something fishy."

"We won't have time." Zandra hoisted the bag over her shoulder, and we headed back toward town, following a worn walking trail through the woods.

"If you don't rest, you'll be forced to," I said. "We can't keep going like this."

"Flat-out crazy seems to be the norm these days," Zandra said. "Everywhere we turn, things are super odd."

As if to prove her point, we'd just stepped onto the main street in Crimson Cove when two individuals bundled out of Vorana Stowell's bookstore, whacking each other over the head with hefty hardbacks, taking turns to slug each other.

Vorana rushed after them, hands raised. "Stop that at once! That's a first edition! It's expensive."

We were heading over to help when a gaggle of imps romped past, haphazardly flaring out magic and causing people to scatter before they got hit with a stinging sparkle.

Zandra got whacked in the chest with an errant blast of imp magic and flew back, landing on her behind and dropping the hedgehogs.

I raced over to her, hissing curses at the imp. "Did anything get broken?"

"My dignity." She winced as she checked for injuries. "How many times will I land on my backside today? I'm not that well-padded."

"What do you say to that break now?" I asked, watching Vorana as she shooed away the troublemakers and collected her stock before heading back inside her bookstore, the books tucked protectively against her chest. "Your buttocks will thank you."

Zandra glowered at me. "I'll have a bruise in a place I don't need a bruise."

"Then you definitely need to rest. And maybe ice your butt. You can't work injured."

Zandra sighed. "Sure. Let's take a break before something gets broken." She checked the hedgehogs were fine and gathered them up.

I walked alongside Zandra, keeping a beady eye out for trouble. I slowed as a large, sleek black limo sputtered and belched its way to a stop in the middle of the road.

It wasn't often we got limousines in Crimson Cove. Few people drove regular cars because magic loved to tinker with the mechanics. You had to wield some hefty spells to stop the mechanisms from malfunctioning. Someone must have forgotten to tell that to the limo driver.

"Do we have a celebrity in town?" I asked.

"That's the last thing we need," Zandra said. "If a celebrity gets swallowed up by our misbehaving magic, it'll bring the authorities to our door. And the media. Yuck."

As we walked past the limo, the back door opened, and several attractive women tumbled out, twittering and complaining. They wore similar outfits of fitted jeans and jackets. Their vests were sparkly and tight.

They walked around the limo several times, not seeming to know what to do. Eventually, a harried driver in a crumpled black suit, wearing a flat cap, got out, stood in front of the limo, and scratched his belly, exposing a hairy gut.

"Let's get out of here before they ask us for help," Zandra muttered.

I followed her as we headed toward animal control. "We should put up a sign at the entrance to town. All ye beware: magic malfunctions are a common occurrence. Enter at your peril."

"But why is it going so wrong?" Zandra asked. "Crimson Cove attracts powerful magic users, but most of us know how to handle our powers. What's messing up the balance?"

"It's been messed up since the attack on Randal and his friends," I said.

"It was wonky before that." Zandra wrinkled her nose.

Randal was still a sore spot after they'd fallen out during a recent investigation involving his friends and Zandra's older half-sister, Tempest. Zandra hadn't spoken to Randal since, even though they both worked for animal control.

"Randal's friend, Charlie, is still in a magically induced coma," I said. "The doctors have given up trying to fix him. Even your Granny Dottie couldn't figure out what was wrong with him, and she poked and prodded him for hours."

"She was furious about failing," Zandra said. "Granny Dottie hates to be defeated, but she went through all her spell books and tried dozens of things to wake Charlie. Nothing worked."

"I feel sorry for the guy," I said. "He has no idea what's going on. He may not even know one of his friends is dead."

"Maybe he'll wake once the town's magic is fixed," Zandra said. "It could be interfering with the doctors' attempts to heal him."

I nodded. I should spend more time looking into the troubles affecting the town. If it got worse, Crimson Cove wouldn't be safe. It had always been on the spicy side, but this was a tabasco-fueled magic issue with a side order of ghost chili.

We entered animal control and were met with the chaotic noise of too many animals and stressed-out staff. Barney was yelling at someone in his office, so we skipped past and went to the back of the building, where the animal pens were housed. We found an empty pen, and Zandra carefully extracted the three sleeping hedgehogs, placing them inside and ensuring the pen was secure with magic to keep them contained.

"Everyone seems anxious today," I noted as I inspected the pens. We had a myriad of magical creatures in holding, and they all looked terrified, ears flat, eyes wide. A few were panting.

"They're anxious about something." Zandra yanked off her gloves. "But we don't have time to figure out what their problem is. There'll be a pile of jobs waiting on the desk with our names on it."

"It's the end of our shift," I said. "They'll wait until the morning."

"Zandra! Juno!" Barney appeared in the doorway. Perched on his shoulder was his familiar, Ember Dreamscape, a chirpy little cat with an optimistic outlook on life. "Finally caught those gassy little pricklers, I see."

"Not without getting a few bruises along the way," I said. "At least that's one trio of problems off the street."

Barney was a bear of a man—broad-shouldered, ruddy-cheeked, and gruff, though he had a soft center. "Good work. But there's still so much to do."

"We can keep working if you want us to," Zandra offered.

Barney hesitated, clearly torn between keeping the streets safe and ensuring his staff didn't collapse with exhaustion. "No, you head home. It's late, and you've already pulled a double shift. You've been pulling them all week. I am grateful. Once this chaos dies down, I'll sort you extra vacation time. We'll all need a well-deserved break after this."

"If you're sure." Zandra looked visibly relieved. My witch never enjoyed admitting she was operating on fumes and needed to recharge. She saw it as a sign of weakness.

"Absolutely," Barney said. "I've pulled together extra funds, and we've got staff from out-of-town coming to lend a hand. We'll get this under control soon. Off you go now. I don't want to see either of you until tomorrow."

I was happy to leave work. I enjoyed helping, but I had to keep an eye on my witch. She was terrible at looking after herself, and I didn't want her getting run down.

"Let's go to the bar," Zandra said. "I could do with one of their enormous greasy burgers and a beer."

"They do a good shrimp cocktail," I said.

"Then it's a plan."

After finishing some paperwork, we left animal control and hurried along the street, keeping a watchful eye out for trouble. We passed the limo again, but it hadn't moved. The driver must have gone to find help.

We'd taken a dozen steps past the limo when the engine roared to life, and the vehicle sped toward us.

Chapter 2

Haunted limo

The snarling limo was determined to run us down. Every time we dodged or changed direction, the limo did the same.

"We should split up," I shouted. "You get to high ground where it's safe."

"There's no way I'm letting that limo run you down." Zandra flung a spell over her shoulder, which pinged ineffectively off the limo's shiny roof.

"Aim for its tires! We need to disable it."

"That's what I was aiming for."

I leaped on a huge industrial trash container left out for collection and thrust a spell toward the limo. My magic spattered around it like damp confetti. The limo smashed into the trash container, sending me sprawling and filling the air with enraged hisses.

I shook out a paw and took off after Zandra. My magic often misbehaved, but recently, I didn't know what I'd be blasting out. It was letting me down when we needed it the most.

The limousine roared like a wild beast, tires screeching as it lunged straight for us. Its polished black body gleamed, and jagged arcs of magic crackled across the hood like lightning looking for something to fry.

"Zandra, move!" I yowled, fur bristling as I darted sideways, barely avoiding being flattened.

Zandra flung up her hands, purple sparks flying from her fingertips, aimed at the limo.

Nothing happened.

The limo veered hard, nearly clipping people who'd foolishly stopped to watch the show, then bore down on us again, headlights flashing like furious eyes.

I flattened my ears. There had to be a way to stop this hexed vehicle.

Zandra's breath hitched as she fumbled for another spell. When did my wonderful witch ever fumble her magic? A swirl of light shot toward the limo then bounced off the windshield and smacked into a nearby lamppost. The iron pole glowed red-hot then exploded in a shower of sparks.

I hissed and leaped aside, avoiding the stinging sparks.

The limousine skidded sideways, tires smoking. There was no one behind the wheel, but the steering wheel jerked like an invisible force had its hands wrapped around it.

It attacked again, its chrome grille wide like the maw of a hungry beast.

Zandra slashed a hand through the air, and a thick, glowing rope shot from her hands, looping around the front bumper.

"Yes!" I cheered, until the limo yanked back as it reversed direction with three times the strength, dragging Zandra with it.

"Bad idea! Bad idea!" she shrieked as she was hauled off her feet and dragged through the air.

My heart slammed against my ribs. "Let go of the rope!"

"I can't." She flailed, boots barely skimming the road. "My hands are stuck."

I launched myself, murder mittens extended, onto the limo's roof. The moment my paws hit the metal, a shockwave of dark energy sent me flying.

I hit the ground and rolled to a stop in the middle of the street, dazed. When I lifted my head, the limousine was bearing down on me.

A searing pain shot through my tail as the tire rolled over it. A strangled yowl ripped from my throat. The world blurred. My perfect tail. Why was my tail always a target?

"Juno!" Zandra's voice cut through my haze. She'd somehow stopped the limo and sprinted toward me, eyes wide with panic.

I bared my teeth, tail throbbing.

The limousine revved again, preparing for another charge.

Zandra's expression hardened. She planted her feet, thrusting her hands high. A storm of pink-and-blue sparks exploded from her hands. The air crackled. The limousine shuddered and then collapsed in on itself until it was the size of a soup can.

I lay panting, not strong enough to look at the damage caused to my tail.

Zandra crouched beside me, wincing. "I am so, so sorry. I thought I had it under control. I planned to lasso it like it was an angry horse and bring it to heel. It wasn't supposed to take its anger out on you."

"Oh, my goodness! Your poor kitty isn't dead, right?" A woman I'd seen get out of the limousine raced toward us, her arms full of bags of candy and a large feather boa wrapped around her neck, tangled in her brunette hair. "Someone said a car lost control. I looked out the store window and realized it was our hired limousine! When we got the rental, we didn't ask for one with a killer personality."

"Thankfully, I'm very much alive," I said.

"Your tail doesn't look so good." Zandra leaned over me, her face even paler than usual as she stared at my still throbbing tail.

"What's going on?" A second dark-haired witch, who looked eerily similar to the first, joined us. She had a pink, sparkly feather boa around her neck and held an inflatable flamingo.

"Our limousine tried to squash this pretty kitty cat," the first woman said. "I knew there was something wrong with that thing when the driver couldn't get the tunes pumping. We hired a haunted limo!"

Zandra ignored their twittering and held her hands over my damaged tail. "You'll be fine. We've dealt with way worse than this. Nothing that a few healing spells and a plate of smoked salmon can't fix." Her magic shimmered over me, but it lacked its usual intensity, and my tail still painfully pulsated.

"I'll need at least two plates." I gritted my teeth as the pain grew worse.

"How does that feel?" Zandra asked, a line of concentration etched between her eyebrows.

"Like I've been run over by a limousine." I didn't mean to sound grouchy, but you try having one of your most precious limbs squished, and you'd feel the exact same way.

Zandra stared at her palms. "I'm using the right healing spell, but it doesn't want to come out. Every time I cast something, it does almost the opposite. My magic feels drained, as if it's fighting itself. I've never felt anything like it."

The ground shook as running footsteps approached.

"Hey! What are you two doing standing around?"

"Yeah, wiggle those beautiful butts. We have partying to get started."

A tall, blonde beauty with huge pink, glossy lips, and a small, wiry woman with a blonde pixie cut and painted-on jeans joined their friends. They also had feather boas wrapped around them.

"We're trying to help this cat," the first dark-haired woman said, a witch if her magical energy was accurate. "I feel gross that she got herself squished by our silly car. Is there anything we can do to help? Does she like candy? Candy always makes me feel better when I'm in a huff about something."

"She does not," I said. "Unless it's fishy."

"Give us some space," Zandra snapped, never easy around strangers.

The witch ignored her and inched closer. "Emiline is great at healing spells. Emiline, drop the supplies and come see what you can do."

The witch with the short blonde hair ignored Zandra's furious glare and kneeled beside me. She smelled of apples and donuts. It was a pleasant combination.

Her eyes widened a fraction. "Wow. I sense your power. You can't heal yourself?"

"I can heal, but my magic has been... testy lately," I said. "And my wonderful witch, Zandra Crypt, the most powerful, all magical, most incredible witch you'll ever have the honor of meeting, is weary after a long day of work."

"I don't have to worry about that." Emiline cracked her knuckles. "We've been sitting in the back of a limousine drinking champagne for hours. My magic is primed and ready to go. I can help if you want me to."

"How can we trust you?" Zandra asked. "You just tried to murder my familiar!"

"Not us! Thelma, tell her. We're good witches," the younger dark-haired witch said.

"That's enough," the older brunette, Thelma, said with an eye-roll. "Agatha loves to make a song and dance out of everything."

"So I should when a kitty's life is on the line."

"It's not on the line." Emiline was staring at my tail. "But that's got to hurt."

"Emiline works at the magic rehab center in Graves Rouge," Thelma said. "She has the healing touch."

"I've heard of that place." Zandra's expression grew slightly less frosty. "You help magic users who are beyond saving."

"Most say beyond saving, but I only see a problem that hasn't had the correct solution applied," Emiline said. "And I can certainly handle one squashed cat's tail."

"What do you think, Juno?" Zandra asked.

"You have my permission to cast magic on my tail," I said to Emiline.

"Thank you. I always seek permission before casting any spells."

"Because it's too easy to get sued these days," Thelma said with a smirk.

Emiline set down the bulging bag she had slung over one shoulder, out of which poked several boxes of cake, held her hands over my tail, and cast a warm wave of magic that made me want to close my eyes.

"That feels wonderful. You do have the healing touch," I said.

"That's what I'm paid for," Emiline said. "I can fix most physical injuries, but it's the ones up top that take the extra effort."

"How long have you worked at Graves Rouge?" Zandra asked.

"I started there as an intern and never left. Going on ten years," Emiline said. "That place gets under your skin. Everyone thinks magic is an incredible tool that fixes all problems, but it's not that simple. Sometimes, magic does more harm than good."

I groaned slightly as her wonderfully warm, soothing magic repaired my tail. "We've been having a few problems like that in Crimson Cove. The magic is going haywire."

"It's not a problem with your ley lines, is it?" Agatha had crept closer while Emiline worked her magic. "That's why we're here. Well, the ley lines and the delicious vampires that live in Oak Park Ridge. Those guys are yummy."

"And bitey," Emiline said. "Agatha's mind is only ever on two things—parties and hot guys."

"Hey! That's not fair," Agatha said. "I sometimes think about what to eat for dinner."

Thelma nudged her with the toe of her sparkling black boot. "And family. You'll never forget me."

"Sisters?" I asked, partly to take my mind off the intense tingling in my tail.

"That's right. Thelma is the sensible one," Emiline muttered as she continued healing me.

"Allegedly," Thelma said. "One of us has to be."

"Wherever Agatha goes, Thelma's not far behind, making sure she doesn't get in too much trouble." Emiline smiled and winked at me.

"Not true. It's because I know the best parties," Agatha said, "and I'm happy for my big sister to tag along, so long as she doesn't embarrass me or make me go to bed too early."

"You're the one who always embarrasses me," Thelma said. "You always say dumb things whenever you see a hot guy you like the look of."

"Is there a problem with your ley lines?" the other blonde witch, who'd not spoken yet, asked.

"As far as I'm aware, they're working to perfection," I said.

"Good. These three want to party, but I'm here for the pure magic. I heard Crimson Cove's ley lines are something else."

"You'd never think we were all best friends," Emiline said as she stroked another calming wave of healing magic across my tail. "Agatha and Thelma are party girls, whereas Clementine loves her supernatural history." She tilted her chin to the second blonde witch.

"What about you?" I asked. "Where do you fit?"

"Emiline's the smart one," Agatha said, with a small nose wrinkle. "At least, that's what she tells us."

"I don't need to tell you. I show you," Emiline said, leaning back. "How do you feel?"

"My tail has never felt so good," I said. "Those hands work miracles."

"These hands have had many years of healing tough cases. It was a pleasure to treat such a simple injury. If you have any trouble with it, just come find me. We're staying on Lady Luck Avenue in a rental. We'll be here a couple of days."

"I want at least a week with those vampires," Agatha said. "One is never enough."

"We really are sorry about the limo," Thelma said. "We don't know what went wrong with it. It started acting strange when we crossed your town border."

"I blame the hire company," Thelma said.

"They gave us a dud vehicle. I'll insist on a refund," Agatha added. "But I need to find that jerk of a driver before I can do that. He slunk off when he realized he couldn't fix the engine."

"I wouldn't blame the limo driver," Zandra said. "Crimson Cove's magic isn't friendly to vehicles that don't have the proper wards around them."

"Oh! Why didn't I think of that?" Emiline said. "This town is full of powerful magic, so of course, it'll mess with anything non-magical. Agatha, did you take out the proper ward insurance?"

"Um... I don't remember. I glazed over when the sales guy started saying something about extra coverage. He might have mentioned wards, but it was so dull. And expensive."

The group groaned, and Thelma shoved Agatha in the shoulder.

Clementine turned sharply, her shoulders lifting. "Does Crimson Cove always feel like this?"

"What are you sensing?" I asked.

"A weird vibe. Could it be your ley lines?"

I turned my attention away from my perfect tail and tuned into the town's magic. I couldn't sense anything odd. Well, no odder than usual.

"I'm sensing nothing strange," Agatha said. "But if it means you come party with the vampires rather than wander about in the woods getting lost like you usually do, then there's definitely something wrong with the ley lines, and you should stay away from them. They could wrap around you and choke the life from you."

Clementine made a noise of exasperation in her throat, although she still looked pensive.

"Let Clementine do what she wants," Emiline said.

"Emiline, you've yet to decide who you plan to party with," Agatha said. "You're welcome to hang out with the vampires, drinking champagne and being sweet-talked, or go get bored and cold with

Clementine while she tackles the town's evil ley lines."

"Ley lines are never evil." Clementine shook out her hands. "It's probably nothing. I'm just sensitive."

Agatha jabbed Emiline in the arm. "Whose party are you joining?"

"Not yours if you keep being so annoying," Emiline said.

"What's with all the party supplies?" I inspected the bulging bag of treats and the inflatable flamingo.

"We have a genius plan," Agatha said. "Vampire clans rarely let in strangers unless they know we're seriously attached to a guy."

"If we have long-term boyfriends, it's supposed to stop us from falling dangerously in love with the vamps and never leave." Thelma rolled her eyes. "We're only here for a good time, not a long time. I don't want to marry a vampire. Just, you know, fool around with one for a while. Besides, I kinda have someone, but what he doesn't know won't hurt him."

Agatha nodded along. "Me, too. But it's not like we're married. Anyway, we came up with the idea that we're here for a hen party, and Thelma is getting married next week. Then the vampires won't worry about us getting all doe-eyed and obsessed."

"And the rest of us are wearing engagement rings." Emiline shook her head as she flashed a fake diamond ring. "The vampires won't buy it. They'll beguile us, get the truth, then kick us out the front door."

"We know Remus Salamander. We could put in a good word for you," I said. "Call it a thank you for fixing my tail."

"Juno," Zandra muttered.

"You'd do that for us?" Agatha's expression brightened. "We've been trying to get access to this hive for ages. They always turn us down."

"We're friendly with Remus and his hive," I said. "Although I'd advise you to be careful of Remus's hellhound. He can be boisterous."

"A hellhound!" Agatha exclaimed. "I bet he's a cutie."

"Oh, he's rarely described as cute, but he enjoys a belly rub," I said.

As the friends gathered their supplies and chatted about getting in with the vampires, Zandra leaned in close to me. "Remus won't thank us for sending a bunch of twittering strangers to his door."

"We've barely seen Remus lately," I said. "He'll appreciate us sending him these bundles of sparkling fun to enjoy."

"And what if that fun ends up getting drained?"

"He'd never do such a thing. Well... maybe he'll take a gentle nibble, but they'll come out the other side unharmed," I said.

"You'll get in trouble," Zandra warned.

"Worse trouble than having an enchanted, hexed limousine run over my tail? That topped up my trouble meter for at least a week."

Zandra shrugged, shaking her head as I told the witches where to find Remus and assured them I'd put in a word before they showed up on his doorstep with their flamingo and feather boas.

Then, with friendly goodbyes and air kisses from the fake hen party, they headed off.

"I just saw Vorana go into the café," Zandra said. "Let's find out why those guys were fighting over a book."

We headed into Sorcha Creer's café and discovered Vorana clutching a large mug of hot chocolate with a generous topping of mini melted marshmallows and squirty cream. Surprisingly, Sage wasn't with her.

"Greetings! What happened to the guys beating themselves senseless with your priceless books?" I hopped onto the table, but Sorcha gently shooed me off.

Vorana groaned and hid her head in her hands for a few seconds, her dark hair acting like a curtain. "Who would have thought books could become lethal weapons? Those idiots came in asking for a book on antique magical lanterns, and the next thing, they're arguing over who buys it. Before the fight started, they'd been acting like the best of friends, geeking out over the store and everything they wanted to buy. It was as if someone zapped them with an evil spell."

"There's a lot of that going around." Zandra grabbed her own hot chocolate. She also got a dried fishy treat Sorcha kept in stock since she often fostered unwanted magical creatures.

"What's been going on with you?" Vorana asked.

"We just had a near miss with a hexed limousine," I said.

"Come again?" Sorcha asked, her freckled nose wrinkling.

"We met four witches who are here to enjoy the ley lines and our vampire hunks," I said. "They cruised into town in a hired limo, which went wrong. When we walked by, it sprang to life and ran over my tail."

"The limo attacked you?" Vorana looked at my now perfect tail.

"It didn't attack. We were just in the wrong place at the wrong time," Zandra said.

"It seemed intent on destroying me," I said.

"What about the driver?" Vorana asked. "Couldn't they control it?"

"Missing in action," I replied. "Where's Sage?"

"Sleeping. The last time she saw the kittens, they had a serious run-in. They're small, but they have so much power. I had to separate them before it got out of control. Sage's fur still looks singed."

"I'll get them a new home as soon as I find somewhere suitable," I said. "Work has been so busy that I've not had a moment to myself, and I need to make sure they go to the right family, especially since their magic needs work."

"I know you're doing your best," Vorana said, "but Sage has threatened to move out if those kittens don't leave by the end of the month."

"I'll get on it tomorrow," I said.

"We were heading to the bar," Zandra said. "After the day we've had at animal control, I need to wind down. Why don't you close early and join us?"

"I may as well, since it's a quiet evening," Sorcha said. "Although I've got a problem with my freezer again, so I should fix that. But I patched it up, so it'll hold until the morning. Everything else can wait until tomorrow." Just as Sorcha was about to flip the closed sign, a gaggle of hungry customers arrived. "Or maybe not."

"How about you?" Zandra asked Vorana. "Have you had enough of book-wielding maniacs?"

"I need to go back to the bookstore, tidy the mess, then I'm heading home to check on Sage. She's got me worried. She even turned down lunch, and she never misses a meal."

"I'll check in on her when we get back later," I said. "Just keep the kittens away from her. She despises them."

"Don't I know it! Although they haven't been around much," Vorana said. "I guess they're testing their independence."

"Which will make Sage happy," I said. "But they're too small to be out on their own all the time. I'll look out for them when we head through town. Make sure they're not up to mischief."

"If you change your minds, you know where we'll be," Zandra said.

We left the café, enjoying a leisurely stroll to the bar on the edge of town. It was next door to Torin Connor's repair shop, which had already closed for the evening.

The second Zandra pushed open the door to enter the bar, loud music hit us.

As I took in the surprisingly sizeable crowd, I groaned. At the bar, the four witches from the rampaging limousine were lining up shots and demanding the music be turned up.

So much for a chilled evening off.

Chapter 3

Fun times

Zandra staggered out of the bar, yelling a slurred goodbye over her shoulder and almost losing her footing and eating dirt.

"Those girls sure know how to dance," she said. "My shirt is soaked through with sweat. That's my kind of workout."

I chuckled to myself. That had more to do with the bottles of champagne our new friends had opened, one of which got sprayed all over Zandra. Not that she minded, at least not after her fifth shot. Or was it her seventh?

My wonderful witch wasn't a drinker, but she'd made up for it this evening. Our witchy companions had been generous, insisting they pay for everything to make up for my injured tail. So, we'd joined in the fun. Hours of drinking, flirting with random strangers, and even dancing on the bar.

It was good to see Zandra let her hair down. We all had issues, but hers had been getting on top of her recently, and I'd been worried she'd gotten stuck in a funk with no sign of an exit.

"That was just what we needed," I said. "Even my paws are sore from all the dancing."

"Those girls are fun." Zandra weaved her way along the street.

I walked beside her, keeping to the roadside to ensure she didn't stagger in front of an oncoming vehicle.

"Emiline has sass," I said. "The sisters are funny. And even Clementine was amusing when she let her guard down."

"Remus and his vampires won't know what's hit them when they show up demanding gorgeous vampires to smooch," Zandra said.

"We'll make sure he looks after them," I said. "That reminds me. We must send him a message so he welcomes them in."

"I'll do it now." Zandra fumbled her mobile snow globe out of her pocket and dropped it. "Oopsie! I've had way too many shots. This fun won't feel so good in the morning when we have to get up for work."

"Let me fix that." I conjured a spell and shot it at Zandra. Rather than spreading over her, it bounced off her forehead with a loud ping and knocked her over.

"Hey! What was that for?" she yelped as she rolled around, one hand clutching her forehead.

I jumped onto her chest and licked the end of her nose. "My apologies. I used a hangover spell to get rid of tomorrow's headache. It must have messed up."

"Whatever that was, it wasn't a hangover spell." Zandra rubbed her forehead then burst into laughter. "Do you remember that guy who got hold of the inflatable flamingo? He rode it around the bar for half an hour, making those weird duck noises."

"And prodding ladies in the bust with its beak. It ended up in the toilet," I said. "Deflated."

Zandra lifted me onto her shoulder before staggering to her feet. "We should get their numbers and stay in touch."

"I agree. But pick up your mobile, or you won't get any new numbers or have access to any old ones."

"Huh! Oh, there it is." Zandra accidentally kicked the mobile snow globe, and it slid away. "Hey! Come back here, you."

"We need more fun in our lives." I held back laughter as Zandra kept chasing and missing her mobile. "Things get so serious when we're always working. And now you've put the nail in the coffin of your romance with Randal..."

"There was never a romance to be had." Zandra grabbed the mobile and held it up in triumph. "And the last time I spoke to him, he said he'd found a new job. He's moving on from animal control. It's for the best."

"You're happy about him going?" I asked. "I know he's made mistakes, but he's sweet and considerate of your needs."

"It's too complicated," Zandra said. "And you know my lack of dating history. If we tried anything, we'd only mess up. It's easier this way."

"So long as you're happy," I said.

"How can I be unhappy when I've got you?" Zandra grabbed hold of a lamppost to stop herself from falling. "You and all your secrets."

I tensed. "My secrets?"

Zandra wiggled her fingers in the air. "Yeah. Let's talk about them."

"Or you could send a message to Remus to let him know about our new friends."

Zandra pursed her lips. "Haven't I already done that?"

"Almost. You dropped your snow globe before you typed anything."

She peered down at her mobile globe and furiously tapped away. Some of the words even made sense. "Done!"

I narrowed my eyes, an unpleasant odor drifting over us. "Something is watching us."

"Uh-uh. You're not getting out of this. You can make all the excuses you like, but I know you keep secrets. And I know you used magic on me to ensure I forgot something important. Well, tough luck, kitty. I remember everything."

"That's delightful. But we need to move." My hackles lifted, and I growled. "There's definitely something watching us." The unstable magic in the air made my whiskers spark and twitch.

"Is it the hexed limo creeping back for a second go?" Zandra giggled. "Let me at it. I'll turn it into a tin can again."

That's when I heard it. The slow scrape of claws on the road and a rumble of growls that came from everywhere at once. My night vision caught them first. Three massive shapes emerging from the shadows, bigger than any dog had a right to be. Their eyes glowed like burning embers.

"Oh, stars and shadows," I hissed. "Zandra, we need to run. Now!"

She finally sensed the danger, stumbling into a defensive stance. She raised her hands. Magic crackled between her fingers and turned her hair bright blue instead of creating the shield she'd intended.

The largest dog-like creature lunged. I fired a stinging spell at it, leaping off Zandra's shoulders and standing in front of her to keep her safe. The beast howled and stopped its attack.

"Run!" I repeated, head-butting Zandra in the leg until she stirred into action.

We bolted toward town, the dogs' snarls echoing off the buildings, their massive paws thundering behind us, making the ground shake.

Zandra cast a spell over her shoulder, but whatever she was planning, it transformed into a shower of sparkling butterflies that flittered around the dogs.

The middle dog leaped. I tried to dodge its impact, but it was fast. Teeth like ice-cold daggers sank into my left haunch. Pain exploded through my body. I screeched, instinctively casting a protection charm that backfired spectacularly and only seemed to stun the dog for a second. But it was enough to make it let go and give me a chance to retaliate.

My cry of pain cut through Zandra's drunken haze. She spun around, eyes blazing with sudden clarity. "Get away from Juno!" She punctuated each word with a blast of pure force that worked, sending the dogs tumbling back and giving us time to flee.

Zandra lifted me, and we sped toward Vorana's house. But the dog-like critters recovered quickly, their howls growing closer again.

One flanked left while another went right, trying to cut off our escape and stop us from reaching safety. The largest stayed directly behind, its massive jaws snapping at us.

"We're almost there!" Zandra gasped. She fumbled with her key, dropping it twice before getting it in the lock. The dogs closed in from three sides, their red eyes blazing with triumph, thinking they had us cornered.

I gathered my magical energy and spat it at them in a furious hiss of light and power, which I focused on making into a blast of lightning. Instead, I turned their fur polka-dotted. They didn't even slow.

We crashed through the front door, and Zandra slammed it shut. The house's protection wards rebuffed the dogs' attack on the door. They howled their fury, crackling with dark energy as they tried to break through. The wards held, barely, glowing bright blue against the darkness.

"That was way too close. Why did they want to eat us?" Zandra was slumped on the floor, holding me against her chest.

"Another case of wrong place, wrong time?" My haunch throbbed, and I let out a pitiful meow. I rarely meowed.

"Let me see that bite." Zandra's voice was steadier now as adrenaline burned away the alcohol.

The wound throbbed with unnatural cold, and I could feel whatever dark magic had been in those teeth spreading through my blood. "Make it quick."

Outside, the dogs continued their assault on our barriers.

"That looks bad!" Zandra cradled me against her chest after she'd looked at my injury.

"I could be brave and say it's only a flesh wound, but we need to remove whatever magic was in that bite."

"I smell blood!" Sage drifted down the stairs without her harness, using magic to float a few inches off the floor. "Who's injured?"

"Juno got bitten," Zandra said.

"You're dripping blood all over Vorana's wooden floor!" Sage's usually pristine fur looked wiry, and she was missing several patches.

"What happened to you?" I asked.

"As if you don't know." Sage sighed. "Those kitten menaces. Come through to the kitchen. The floor is easier to clean in there."

Zandra hurried into the kitchen, still clutching me to her chest.

"What chased you?" Sage asked.

"It looked like a pack of wild dogs," Zandra said, "but they had glowing red eyes."

"Hellhounds? Archie's friends?"

"If they are, I've never seen them before," I said. "And they were anything but friendly."

Zandra set me on the kitchen table. Sage floated beside me, waiting until I was settled before inspecting my wound. She hissed out a breath.

"A nasty puncture wound on your back leg," she muttered. "A deep bite. It smells bad."

"They weren't playing," Zandra said.

"Fetch the stack of poultice wraps Vorana keeps in the cupboard under the stairs, along with the tin box with the gold star on top," Sage said.

Zandra dashed off.

"There's no need to fuss," I said. "A few magic spells, and I'll be fine."

"Except you won't," Sage said. "You know magic has been acting strangely, and we both sense the bite contains gross darkness. I've been avoiding casting spells because they keep going wrong. And I'm always exhausted. I know it's a sign of old age, but it's also a sign Crimson Cove is broken."

I grudgingly nodded. "I wondered if there was a problem with the ley lines."

"I'll tell you what the problem is," Sage said. "Those kittens! Ever since they showed up, trouble has focused on us."

"Those adorable fluff babies have nothing to do with this," I said. "Don't let your jealousy do the talking."

"I may be jealous, but I also know when there's a problem," Sage said. "And it's living under this roof. And I'm not talking about you or Zandra."

"Are the kittens here at the moment?"

"Thankfully not," Sage said. "After our last encounter, I told them if I ever saw them again, they'd be sorry. I'd show them my true power and turn them into marshmallows then stomp on them until they were squishy."

"That was unnecessarily violent. What did they do?"

"Laughed at me."

"They have a ridiculous level of cheekiness," I said. "I remember what I was like as a youngster—"

"Here we are," Zandra said as she returned, setting down the tin box and the poultice wraps.

"Combine the green paste with the red gel into an ointment. That should do the trick," Sage said. "But it'll take overnight to heal."

Zandra did as Sage instructed, carefully wrapping my injured leg in the sticky, stinky poultice.

"I think the dogs have finally backed off. I don't hear them howling."

"We're safe," I said.

Sage grumbled. "Until you bring the next calamity to our door."

A loud and unwelcome banging jerked me from my restorative sleep.

I sat up sharply then winced. My back leg throbbed a warning. The magical poultice hadn't quite finished doing its job.

Zandra was bleary-eyed as she stared at me. "Who is that at this unnatural hour?"

I hopped off the sofa. We'd slept in the living room to watch for the crazed dogs to make sure they didn't get inside, but there'd been no sign of them, and we'd eventually dozed off.

"Hold on a minute. I'm coming. If you damage my front door, I'll make you buy me a new one." Vorana passed the living room, tying the belt on her robe. She backtracked and peered in. "Did you sleep here last night?"

"We thought it best," I said.

There was more hammering on the front door. "I'm sure there's a story behind that comment. Give me a minute. I want to know everything. Just let me get rid of our rude dawn caller."

Zandra stretched and yawned. "How's the leg?"

"Better than last night," I said.

"I'll submit a report when we get to animal control," Zandra said. "If anyone else meets those wild dogs, they may not be as lucky as we were."

"I don't call getting savaged lucky," I said. "And there was something unnatural about those beasts."

"You know what I mean. At least we had a place to run to. Meet those things in the woods, and you'd be a goner."

Cythera interrupted us, stomping into the living room, righteous indignation on her gloriously perfect angel face.

Finn dashed in behind her, looking disheveled. His clothing was rumpled, and he hadn't shaved for days.

Vorana hurried in after them. "They wanted to know where you were and then pushed their way in before I could stop them. Cythera trod on my toes!"

"Greetings!" I said. "Are you here to take us to breakfast?"

Cythera flared her wings. "Do you know Agatha Black?"

"No," Zandra said. "Can we go back to sleep now?"

"Agatha from the bar?" I asked. "Remember, there was a witch called Agatha. She got you dancing on the bar and singing into an empty beer bottle."

Zandra's cheeks flushed. "I don't remember that. Her surname is Black? I don't think we asked for her surname."

"I knew it!" Cythera exclaimed. "I knew you'd be behind this. Everyone said you were there. Finn told me to give you the benefit of the doubt, but I know a truth when it's told."

"What are we behind?" I didn't like the triumphant expression on Cythera's face.

"Agatha Black is dead, and the finger of blame is being pointed at you two. I'm taking you in."

Chapter 4

Here comes trouble

"Dead! There's been a mistake." I hadn't moved from my spot on the comfy couch. "Have you not had your morning coffee? Are you in the wrong house? Or remembering a nasty dream?"

"This has nothing to do with my lack of caffeine," Cythera said. "I know exactly where I am, and this isn't a dream. Although every time I deal with you, it feels like a nightmare."

Zandra stretched her arms above her head and yawned. "You've got your information muddled. When we left the bar last night, Agatha was alive. It's a different witch. I'm sorry someone is dead, but it's not Agatha."

"She's dead!" Cythera said. "Murdered!"

"Can you say, hand on heart, that's true? You have been known to make the occasional error when stressed," I said.

"Which is most of the time," Zandra muttered.

Cythera bared her teeth at me. "Are you suggesting I don't know how to check whether a person is dead or alive?"

"I'll get the coffee on, shall I?" Vorana hovered in the doorway, her hands clasped together.

"No coffee! This isn't a social call. We're here to pick up two criminals."

"Coffee would be great," Finn said. "I've got an aching head and a sandpaper tongue."

"Have you been drinking on the job again?" Cythera swooped a wing at Finn.

He held up a hand, a smirk on his face. "As if I'd do such a thing."

Cythera glowered at him. "Focus on detaining the killers and not your issues."

"Hey! They're not killers. Zandra and Juno help with your investigations. Don't be so quick to judge and don't use a tone that makes you sound like you've just come off a four-day-only water fast." Vorana's look was pointed as she left, a silent warning not to start any trouble and trash her delightful room.

"Let's start with the facts," I said. "And take a seat. All that fluttering makes me anxious."

"It's supposed to. We learned the intimidation stance in training." Finn slouched behind Cythera, an uncharacteristic scowl on his face.

I couldn't be certain because I couldn't get a clear view of him, but there were flickers of Finn's demon energy moving across his wings. Finn had been in control of his demon side for months. It was partly because of the love of a good woman, but mainly because he now believed in himself. What was causing his dark side to peek out?

"If you can't be helpful, wait outside," Cythera snapped at him.

"I'm here! I'm helping," Finn said. "Look, here's Vorana with coffee. I'll deal with that since it's not above my pay grade."

I glanced at Zandra. Finn's reaction suggested he'd had a falling out with Cythera.

"I said I wanted nothing to drink." Cythera waved away Vorana's offered mug of coffee as if she were an incompetent house-elf.

"I made it now, so don't let it go to waste." Vorana set down the tea tray. "And there are cinnamon buns. I warmed them, so they'll be delicious."

Finn grabbed two buns and sank his teeth into one of them.

Cythera dismissed the offer of coffee with an ogre-like grunt, but Zandra grabbed one, and Vorana took her own mug and settled on a nearby chair.

"You shouldn't be here," Cythera said.

"This is her house," I said.

"I'm fine with Vorana hearing anything you have to say," Zandra said. "She knows we had nothing to do with what happened to Agatha, who I'm certain is still alive and kicking."

"We don't even know what is alleged to have happened," I said. "Cythera is being elusive. If you give us more information, we can prove our innocence, and you can hunt for the actual killer."

"If I tell you everything, you'll wiggle out of this," Cythera said.

Zandra shook her head. "This feels like a set-up. Do we need to get legal help?"

Cythera growled out a sigh. "I have eyewitness accounts about trouble between you, Agatha, and her friends. Now Agatha is dead. That's not a coincidence."

"I'd call that very much a coincidence," I said. "Although I rarely favor such a thing, this is one such occasion where coincidence wins out. Why not have a cinnamon bun and soothe your anger with sugar and caffeine?"

"Keep your baked goods away from me," Cythera said. "Your kindness won't distract me."

"Cythera! It's a cinnamon bun. It won't make you forget why you came here," Vorana said.

"No bun!" Cythera flapped her wings. "Since you refuse to cooperate, I'm taking you to Angel Force."

"How have we been uncooperative?" I asked. "You can't expect us to confess to a crime we have no knowledge of."

From the sour look on her face, that's exactly what Cythera had expected. Maybe she thought the shocking accusation would make a confession flop out of us. Foolish angel.

"I'm not leaving here till I've finished my coffee and gotten dressed," Zandra said.

Cythera strode across the room and lifted Zandra by the front of her shirt. "I am sick of you and your fluffy fiend messing with Angel Force and assuming you're better than us."

"There was never any assumption. We know we're better." I hissed at Cythera. "And you would be wise to unhand my witch."

Cythera shook Zandra, causing hot coffee to splash everywhere. "Your time in Crimson Cove has brought nothing but chaos. You pretend to help, but everywhere you go, trouble follows. Or, more accurately, you cause it."

"Give us one concrete example that proves we've caused any trouble," I said.

"Zandra's mother turned into a ghoul."

"Not our fault," I said. "And we cracked a case and brought down a criminal gang you'd been after for years. That was a solution, not a problem."

"You keep causing trouble over in Oak Park Ridge and stirring up the vampires," Cythera said. "Remus rarely visited Crimson Cove until you showed up with your weird magic and annoying fluffy face."

I slashed out a murder mitten. "Zandra's face isn't fluffy!"

"Remus is a friend." Zandra got free from Cythera's grip and yanked down her shirt before wiping coffee off the back of her hand. "He visits because we like each other's company."

"You shouldn't mind the vampires. Crimson Cove is friendly to the undead," I said.

"I don't mean their regular comings and goings. I mean the near-death experiences or actual deaths. And let's not get started on the dragons that showed up not so long ago. I lost a valuable member of my team for months."

"You can't blame Finn hiding a dragon's egg on us!" I said. "He got attached to the baby dragon and then fell in love. Two things entirely out of our control."

"You were involved!" Cythera said. "We used to have a quiet, happy town before you rolled up. I've been speaking to my colleague in Willow Tree Falls, and she says the same thing about the rest of your family."

"Stop right there," Zandra said. "You can bad-mouth me all you like but say nothing against my family. The Crypt witches help the angels. That's what we've always done. You need us. Maybe you hate to admit that, but it's the truth. And Crimson Cove has never been full of law-abiding, happy citizens. It's just that you've never noticed them breaking the law until we showed up. Or, more accurately, you turned a blind eye to crime because you were too lazy to solve it and get those wings grubby."

"They have a point, boss," Finn said. "We were always letting stuff slide because we were so busy filling in the paperwork."

"Wait outside," Cythera said.

Finn grinned, grabbed another cinnamon bun, and left the house, slamming the door behind him.

"What have you done to upset Finn?" I asked. "He's usually cheerful."

"I'm making him work for a living. He's not used to it," Cythera said. "You have five minutes, and then I'm dragging you out of this house. Dressed or not." She turned and stamped out of the room.

"Should we make a run for it?" I asked Zandra. "I don't fancy our chances when we get to Angel Force. Cythera must have gotten it wrong about Agatha."

"I've seen Cythera stressed before, but never like this," Vorana said. "Although I heard on the grapevine, they've had more cases than they know what to do with. There have even been visits from the higher angels."

"Uh, oh. They always stir things up," Zandra said. "What are they doing poking around our town?"

"They're looking to improve efficiency numbers and have picked Crimson Cove as a test case."

"No wonder Cythera's in such a foul mood," Zandra said.

I nodded. "Things rarely end well when the higher angels get involved. Perhaps we should offer Cythera an olive branch and answer this ridiculous accusation."

"I don't want to go anywhere with her," Zandra said. "She's already decided we're guilty. Which is wrong. We saw Agatha alive last night."

"Is this the witch that ran you over with the limousine?" Vorana asked.

"Yes, but once we got to know Agatha and her friends, they were fun," I said. "Of course, I was angry after my tail got run over, but Emiline healed me. That's one of Agatha's friends."

"I can't understand why Cythera is saying there were witnesses," Zandra said. "Witnesses to what?"

"Maybe they saw Agatha spray that champagne all over you and thought you weren't happy about it," I said.

"That happened?" Zandra asked.

"You should sniff the clothing you abandoned in the basement," I said. "You smelled like a fancy brewery."

"Huh. I really had way too much to drink last night," Zandra said. "But I'd have remembered if I did anything to Agatha."

"We did nothing. Cythera, as usual, has got the wrong end of the stick. Let's go to Angel Force and sort this," I said. "Then we can look into who died. If it was anyone."

Five minutes later, Cythera hurried us along to Angel Force. She refused to talk or answer the questions we plied her with. Finn was equally unhelpful, although he kept grinning and smirking as if he knew a secret.

As we arrived, two angels blasted out of the main doors, almost knocking us off our feet in their haste to leave. Cythera snarled at them, but they barely paused as they took to the wing.

Inside was a chaotic maelstrom of tension. Angels dashed back and forth, and anxious or angry residents occupied every chair. A wand could have sliced through the uneasy atmosphere.

"This reminds me of animal control," Zandra muttered, stepping out of the way as several angels hurried out the main doors.

"We've had triple the number of crimes reported in the last forty-eight hours," Finn said. "It's been getting worse every day. Cythera's talking about bringing in new recruits to shore things up." He slumped into his chair and spun in it.

"I see you're working hard," I said. "Having a few problems?"

"Nothing I can't handle. Why do you ask?"

"Your demon is showing."

"I don't know what you're talking about," Finn said.

"You don't sense it?"

He shrugged. "I'm tired. It's hard to keep the defenses up. It's Cythera's fault. I worked three shifts back-to-back, and then she dragged me out to pick you up. Thanks for that, by the way. Why don't you make it easy on me and confess?"

"Because we didn't do it," I said. "You know we'd do nothing like that."

"The way the eyewitnesses are talking, you had every reason to want that witch dead," Finn said.

"What eyewitnesses?" Zandra asked. "Give us their names, and we'll make them see sense."

"Let's make this official." Cythera marched past. "We'll take this into an interview room. Finn, you're with me. But behave. No smart comments."

He groaned and rolled his eyes as he dragged himself off his chair.

A few minutes later, we were settled in a private room with Cythera, and Finn sat opposite us. The atmosphere was frostily tense.

Cythera started the interview. "As you know, Agatha Black is dead."

"We only know that thanks to you telling us," I said.

"She was last seen partying with the two of you. What went wrong?"

"Nothing," Zandra said. "We went to the bar to wind down after work and met Agatha and her friends. We hung out. We left before they did, and that was the last time we saw any of them. She's really dead?"

"You argued," Cythera said.

"Not while we were at the bar," I said.

"Earlier in the day. Several people confirmed you confronted a group of witches and things got tense. Are you denying that?"

"There was a misunderstanding over a hexed limousine," I said. "Agatha and her friends hired an unsuitable vehicle to come to town, not realizing how strong our magic is. It broke down. They abandoned the limo at the side of the road. When Zandra and I walked past, the vehicle roared to life and attempted to murder us."

"You're saying you're the victims?" Cythera snorted derisively. "Do you intend to counter-sue?"

"You've lost me," I said. "Who's suing who? Are you suggesting Agatha—who is dead according to you—will sue us from beyond the grave? Are you sure you don't need caffeine?"

Cythera sneered at me. "You aren't clever, and you won't get away with this."

"I am, and there's nothing to get away with," I said. "It's true. After the limousine ran over my tail, the situation became heated. But one of Agatha's friends, Emiline, healed me. We parted on good terms."

"But things went wrong after you met later," Cythera said. "Did Agatha attack first? Perhaps a self-defense plea will shorten your sentence. It's worth a try. Confess you killed Agatha and I may be lenient."

"We arranged nothing, and we attacked no one," Zandra said. "As I already told you, we planned to visit the bar. When we got there, Agatha, her sister

Thelma, and their two friends were already there. They asked us to join them."

"Which, of course, you accepted because you wanted an opportunity to pay them back," Cythera said.

"No, because they offered to pay for everything to make up for the limousine attacking Juno," Zandra said. "When we got to know them, they were fun. That's it. There were no fights. Whoever is telling you they saw us murder Agatha is lying. Go back and ask them why they lied. Maybe they're covering for something they did."

"More than one witness supports this theory," Cythera said.

"Give me their names, and I'll prove they're not telling the truth," I said.

"That's not happening. I knew it was a mistake to trust either of you." Cythera crossed her arms. "Until I figure out exactly what happened, you're staying here."

"You can't do that," Zandra said. "We've done nothing wrong."

"Another lie. Finn, make yourself useful and find them a cell."

Despite our protests, Cythera wouldn't budge and insisted on having us processed.

"How are we supposed to clear our names if we're trapped in a cell?" I asked Finn as he led us away.

Finn winked. "Leave it to me. You won't be stuck in here for long. Just get ready to move." He settled us in one of the few empty cells in Angel Force and left us alone to contemplate this unwelcome outcome.

"What the heck is going on?" Zandra asked. "Cythera seems convinced we murdered Agatha."

"We need to speak to Thelma. She'll set things straight. She was there the whole evening too, so she saw there were no problems between us."

Zandra paced the small cell, her head down and a hand stuffed into her jeans pockets. "I've got to admit, I don't remember much about last night. I did nothing dumb, did I?"

"I remember everything, so I know neither of us did anything wrong unless you count dancing on the bar and singing out of tune."

She winced. "Not my finest hour."

"We'd had a trying day, and you needed to blow off steam. There's nothing wrong with that."

There was more pacing and muttering, but we were at a loss to figure this out. With Cythera determined to bag us for this crime, we could be in serious trouble.

The main door in the corridor swung open, and Finn dashed back in. His demon energy flickered over his feathers, and there was a sharp smile on his face as he unlocked our door.

I stepped in front of Zandra, not liking the gleam in Finn's eyes. "Are you here to help or hinder?"

He chuckled, a deep, low rumble in his chest that sounded more demon than angel. "The way I'm feeling, I have no idea. But for now, I'm getting you out of here. Cythera is driving me mad. Setting you free will tip her nicely over the edge."

"Why would you want to do that?" I asked.

"No time for questions, or don't you want to look at the body of the witch we're so sure you murdered?"

Chapter 5

Cold clues

After Finn snuck us out of our cell, ignoring the protests of other prisoners to do the same for them, he stuffed us inside a tiny cleaning closet, the potent smell of bleach tickling my booping snooter and forcing Zandra to stifle sneezes in my fur. It was a good job I adored my witch. I'd let no one else sneeze on me.

Finn ordered us to wait until he could cause a distraction then he'd get us in to look at Agatha's body.

"Given the mood Finn's in," I said, "I'm worried about the distraction he'll create. Did you see the demon flickers running through his feathers? He's barely in control of his twisted side."

"Something's off with him, just like most other people," Zandra said. "We've been so busy that we've not been paying enough attention to how bad things have gotten. Maybe it's too late to turn things around."

"We can fix anything. We just need to find the source," I said.

Zandra was quiet for several seconds. "You don't think Cythera's right, do you? We arrive in town and everything goes wrong. Does it have to do with our powers? I'm not a true-blood Crypt witch. They taught me how to use their magic and spells, but if that's gotten distorted somehow... I've always been a magical muddle. What if my muddle messed everything up?"

"This has nothing to do with your powers," I said. "You're the most wonderful witch I've ever stumbled across, and I'm grateful every day we met, even though I was trying to destroy you on that occasion. I was struggling with my own magic, but I saw your astonishing potential. It sliced through my struggles like an ice blade and made me realize I'd been doing everything wrong. It was so pure and strong. There is nothing wrong with your magic. Never let anybody tell you that."

She drew in a slow breath. "What... what about your magic?"

The closet door opened. Finn appeared and gestured us out. "Hurry. You won't have much time."

"Is that smoke I can smell?" I asked as we hurried along after Finn.

"I needed all the angels out of the building in one go. Everyone evacuates when the place is on fire." He chuckled to himself. "You should have seen them squeal and run."

"I don't want anybody getting hurt while you help us," Zandra said.

Finn shot her a glare. "Do you want to see this body or not? It's up to you. I'm not bothered if you clear your names. It's no skin off my nose."

"It should be. We're friends," I said.

"Whatever." He led us to the back of the building, where the angels had a small mortuary. As predicted, thanks to Finn's fire, the place was empty apart from a single body lying under a cover.

"Have you done an autopsy yet?" I asked Finn.

"Not yet. Only run the basic checks and tests. There are so many other cases keeping us busy. It's planned for later today."

"What did the basics show you?" I asked.

"We drew a blank. There are no wounds or marks, nothing to show how Agatha died. Just a weird magic. It's fading, though. It won't be here for much longer." Finn flipped back the sheet to reveal Agatha's lifeless body. "Look for yourself if you like. Just make sure you don't leave any evidence. You wouldn't want to implicate yourself by accident. That would be a sad boo-boo."

"Thanks for the warning," Zandra said.

"Let me look," I said. Neither of us enjoyed being around corpses, but I'd rather inspect the body than Zandra. I didn't want her leaving a fingerprint where one shouldn't be and making this situation more complicated.

A quick inspection of Agatha's cold, lifeless form revealed Finn's truth. As soon as I'd entered the room, I'd sensed a strange power. Some kind of gone-off magic. Something that had my toe beans tingling and made me want to get as far away from the body as possible.

"Where was Agatha found?" I asked.

"Outside. Behind the bar where you'd been having fun," Finn said.

"Who found her?"

"A couple snuck out the back for a sneaky make-out session. They literally stumbled over her."

"Didn't Agatha's friends wonder where she was?" Zandra asked.

"We've spoken to them. They claimed it wasn't uncommon for Agatha to sneak off and do her own thing. It usually involved some hot guy she met up with. They called her the wild one in the group."

"Doesn't that seem odd?" I asked. "Your friend disappears on a night out, and no one goes to find her to ensure she's okay."

"Her sister, Thelma, said she always turned up just before they'd leave for the night," Finn said. "It was typical behavior, so there was nothing for them to worry about."

"What time did the couple find her body?" I asked.

"Just after midnight," Finn said. "She hadn't been dead for long when she was discovered."

"We left ten minutes before that," I said. "Now that I think about it, I didn't see Agatha when we were leaving, but it was busy in the bar, so I assumed we just missed her."

"She could have been out the back being attacked while we left," Zandra said.

"Maybe by you," Finn said. "I'm sorry to say, the timings fit. You should keep that information to yourself unless you want Cythera to lock you in a deep, dark dungeon and magically ward it, so you never get out."

"We'll keep it to ourselves, although lying to Cythera is never wise," I said. "How did Agatha's friends react when they learned the news?"

"As you'd expect. Stunned silence. Shock. A few tears. Thelma didn't take it well."

"I imagine not. They seemed close," I said. "Not all sisters are."

"I know all about that. It took me a long time to feel anything mildly sisterly toward Tempest," Zandra said.

"But now you're close," I said. "Sibling troubles can run deep, though. We should investigate their relationship."

Zandra nodded. "What do you make of this strange magic lingering around Agatha's body?"

"I can't figure out what it is," I said. "I don't like it, though. Maybe the tests the angels run will show something useful."

Finn stood by the door, occasionally glancing along the corridor to ensure we wouldn't be caught. "It's time to go. They've just switched off the alarm, so the fire must be out."

"A few more minutes," I said.

"No can do. You don't want me getting caught misbehaving, do you? Cythera will slap me on the wrists again and tell me I've been a bad boy."

I stared at Agatha's pale, lifeless face. Her long, dark hair was splayed out around her. It was so unfair. What had happened? She'd been so full of life. Who would want to do this? And, most importantly, why were they hoping they could pin the crime on us?

"Let us know what the test results reveal," I said, making sure I left no white furs behind as I hopped onto the floor.

"I'll see what I can do. Now run. You'll need a head start before I'm called out to bring you down." Finn's eyes glowed red for a second before he shook his head. "I'm just doing my job. You understand."

"Before we go, where are Agatha's friends staying?" I asked. "I know they're renting a house on Lady Luck Avenue, but we don't know the number. We need to talk to them as soon as possible."

Finn pulled a piece of paper from his pocket and held it out. "That's the address. They rented a place for a couple of days. You'd better hurry. I'll soon be on your tail." He snapped his teeth.

Zandra grabbed the piece of paper, and we hurried toward the back exit of the building.

We slipped outside, and Zandra poked her head out of the alley before swiftly shuffling back. "The angels are going inside. We'll wait until it's all clear. Cythera will blow a gasket when she realizes we've escaped. She'll have everyone chasing us, thinking we're avoiding being charged with Agatha's murder."

"We can't stay here. We'd be powerless. Cythera's not thinking right, and neither is Finn," I said. "We must keep an eye on him. I don't think he was joking when he said he'd hunt us. He'd probably enjoy it, especially if his demon gets control."

"He's one of a dozen problems we need to tackle." Zandra looked back along the alleyway, worry etched on her face. "I'd cast an invisibility spell over us, but it'll probably backfire and double us in size."

"We'll wait a few minutes, then it'll be safe to move," I said. "Once we give Cythera viable suspects, she'll get off our back. And we need to find out why people are throwing our names into the murder mix. It sounds like it was more than one person."

Zandra nodded and peered out of the alley. "We're good to go."

It was only a ten-minute, speedy walk to the rented house where Agatha and her friends were staying, and we made it without being noticed. Rather than knocking on the front door, we crept around the back and looked for a way in.

Zandra was trying the handle on the back door when it was yanked open. Thelma stood there, her eyes wide with surprise. She dropped the mug she held and backpedaled. "Stay away from me!"

"Wait! We need your help," I said.

"You murdered my sister!" she shouted and turned, fleeing through the house.

Zandra looked at me with shock in her eyes. "Thelma thinks we did it, too. We need to get answers from her. And we need to stop her from raising the alarm."

I raced into the house after Thelma. "There's been a mistake. We did nothing to Agatha! We need your help to figure out what happened last night. Nobody's telling us anything useful."

I couldn't find Thelma in any of the downstairs rooms, but then I heard a door slam upstairs. I sprinted up the stairs with Zandra. There was only one closed door, so we stopped outside it.

"I know you're scared," I said. "But you have nothing to fear from us. I assure you, we did nothing to Agatha. We were as shocked as you when we learned what happened."

"And even more shocked when we heard people are saying we did it," Zandra added. "The last time I saw Agatha, she was alive."

"Go away, or I'll call for help," Thelma said, her tone laced with shrill panic. "Emiline and Clementine will be back soon. Then you'll be in trouble."

"Tell us what happened," I said. "We saw your sister's body. Magic killed her."

The door inched open. "How did you see her body? Did you do it? Everyone is saying you did."

"We know," I said. "But this has nothing to do with us. We have connections with Angel Force, and we looked at the evidence."

Thelma's forehead furrowed. "I heard someone say you're connected to the angels."

"We work for them as consultants on their most difficult cases," I said. "They only hire the best. We help bring criminals to justice. We aren't the bad guys."

Thelma was shaking as she gripped the door. "I don't know who to believe. The angel who spoke to us was so convincing. She said she'd bring you in and she'd never trusted you."

"That sounds like Cythera," I said. "She's not thinking straight. This is a mistake."

"Cythera has listened to panicked testimonials and drawn the wrong conclusion about us," Zandra said. "It won't be the first time. But I promise you, we didn't do it. We want to find out who did."

"Or fake evidence to pin it on someone else," Thelma said.

"We liked Agatha," I said.

"You didn't! Not the first time you met."

"Well, your limousine ran over my tail," I said. "I didn't particularly like anyone in that moment. Not even Zandra."

"Did you want revenge?" Thelma asked. "That's what the angel said. She told me you were deceitful and liked to embarrass law enforcement whenever you could."

"That was unprofessional of Cythera," I said. "Her embarrassed feelings are her problem, not ours."

"When we left the bar last night, your sister was alive," Zandra said.

"She disappeared when you two left," Thelma replied.

"We didn't see her. Do you know where she went?" I asked.

"Not for certain. The bar was stifling, so maybe she went to get air. I thought she'd go out the front. Is that when you saw her? You lurked around and—"

"We'd never do that," I interrupted. "Agatha was a good witch. We're sorry this happened, and we want to make things right."

"But... the angel said people saw you. They said there was a fight," Thelma insisted.

"We don't know who's telling that lie," Zandra said. "But it is a lie. You must believe us. We want to find out who did this to Agatha, and we want to clear our names."

"You should go," Thelma said after a few seconds' pause. "I don't know what to think or who to trust."

"Trust us," I said. "We're on the right side of justice. That's why we work with Angel Force."

"How were things between you and Agatha?" Zandra asked.

Thelma jerked back from the door. "What do you mean?"

"You seemed like you were close sisters, but I wondered if there were any problems between you."

"Her death had nothing to do with me." Thelma's eyes narrowed. "Everyone's saying you did it, and I agree with them!" She backed up, opened the window, and screamed.

I glanced at Zandra and shook my head. It was too risky to stay here.

"You're making a huge mistake," I said to Thelma. "Don't believe what people tell you about us."

"Help! Help!" Thelma shrieked. "There are two insane magic users in the house, and they want me dead!"

"Let's get out of here." Zandra scooped me up and settled me on her shoulder before dashing down the stairs and out the back door. Rather than going onto the main street, we jumped over the back fence and hurried through several more gardens.

After a few minutes, we stopped to rest and ensure we weren't being followed.

"None of this makes sense," I said. "Why does everyone think we're guilty?"

Chapter 6

Friends not reunited

"We have to talk to Emiline and Clementine," I said. "Maybe they saw something different. Something that will prove we're innocent."

"Unless they're the ones spreading the rumor we had something to do with it." Zandra kept one hand on my side, her head down as we stuck close to the shadows.

Fortunately, it was a gloomy day in Crimson Cove. In fact, I couldn't remember the last time I'd seen the sunshine. That was another sign things were going wrong in our town.

"This has something to do with the strange magic lingering on Agatha's body," I said. "It's convincing people they saw something that didn't happen."

"We need to find out who wants to put us behind bars," Zandra said. "They must be behind this."

"That could be a long list," I said. "We've been helping Angel Force with their trickiest crimes for a long time."

"We can't turn to Angel Force for help," Zandra said. "Cythera wants to pin this on us and throw away the key."

"Vorana and Sorcha will help," I said. "We can get one of them to bring Clementine and Emiline to the café so we can talk to them."

"It should be the bookstore," Zandra said. "There are gloomy corners in there, so it'll be easier to hide, and it's usually quiet this time of day."

"Vorana's bookstore isn't behaving," I said. "We don't want to risk getting whacked on the head by a flying book."

"Maybe we can hide in Sorcha's kitchen," Zandra said. "Wherever we go, we must decide fast. Time isn't on our side. The second Cythera realizes we're not in that cell, she'll send angels after us."

"Let's start with the café," I said. "We'll gather information and go from there."

It was mid-morning as we entered Sorcha's café, and there were only a few customers around. From the surprised expression on Sorcha's face, I could tell she'd heard the news about us. Without saying a word, she ushered us behind the counter and hid us in the kitchen.

"I thought you'd been arrested! Everyone is saying you're up on a murder charge," she whispered.

"It's a long story," I said. "The short version is we were taken in for questioning, and Cythera shoved us in a cell. She's not happy with us. But we had inside help and got out. We intend to clear our names."

Sorcha smiled. "Finn. I should have known he'd look out for you. But why is everyone saying you killed that witch?"

"Is that what everyone is saying?" Zandra asked. "The first we heard of it was when Cythera barged into Vorana's this morning and demanded we answer her questions."

Sorcha glanced over her shoulder to check we weren't being overheard by customers waiting at the counter for service. "It's all people are talking about. I don't know how word is spreading so fast. Somebody must have seen you being taken into Angel Force."

"We need help," I said. "We've got to talk to Agatha's friends, Emiline and Clementine. We tried her sister, but Thelma was too panicked. She thinks we're guilty too."

"I know who you're talking about," Sorcha said. "They came in here and bought all the sugar donuts yesterday for some party. They were looking for fun."

"And they had it," Zandra said. "We had a great time at the bar."

"It wasn't a great time for that witch. Agatha, did you say?"

I nodded. "There's twisted magic afoot. We got a quick look at Agatha's body and found an unpleasant spell on her skin, but it was fading. Whoever is doing this is covering their tracks."

"I'll help in any way I can," Sorcha said. "What do you need me to do?"

"Send a message to Vorana while we hide out here. She must find Emiline and Clementine and bring them here so we can talk." Zandra gave Sorcha the rental information and descriptions of the witches, so Vorana would easily identify them.

"While I do that, look at my freezer again," Sorcha said to me. "It's got that weird glitch. The one you had to remove the last time. You know, all that sticky magic."

While Sorcha sent the message to Vorana, I yanked off the nasty magic web around the freezer and tossed it away. "That shouldn't have come back."

"Vorana's on it," Sorcha said. "She's closing the bookstore. I sent her the address where they're staying, so she'll stop them before they go in and convince them to come to the café."

Thirty minutes later, and after a round of hot chocolate, a cherry scone for Zandra, and a plate of smoked salmon for me, Vorana appeared with Clementine and Emiline.

Both witches looked like they'd barely slept. Their eyes were red, and dark rings bruised their skin. The second Emiline saw us, she scowled, lifting her hands, magic sparking on her fingertips.

"What are they doing here?" Clementine whispered. "I thought the angels arrested them."

"They made a mistake," I said. "And we come in peace."

"There's nothing peaceful about you two," Emiline said. She shot a glare at Vorana. "You said Angel Force needed us here. I thought it was weird they wanted to meet in a café."

Vorana gave an apologetic shrug. "I needed to get you to follow me."

Zandra tensed beside me as more magic bloomed around Emiline. "We don't want to fight."

Emiline's eyes blazed with tear-speckled rage. "Too bad. You killed Agatha! If the angels won't deal with you, we will." She hurled a bolt of red magic at Zandra's chest.

I leaped, fur bristling, as I swiped a paw through the energy. It fizzled out, but Clementine was already moving. A shimmering net shot toward me. I twisted, barely dodging it in time as it slammed into a table, turning it into a pile of charred wood.

The few customers in the café raced out before they got embroiled in the fight. Sensible plan.

Zandra flicked her fingers, summoning a spell that shot toward Emiline. Emiline ducked and slammed a palm against the floor. The tiles under Zandra's feet cracked, swirls of energy lashing up to trap her ankles.

"Stop! You're wrecking my café," Sorcha yelled.

Emiline and Clementine ignored her as another volley of magic came at us.

Zandra snapped her fingers, and the swirls of energy exploded into harmless sparks.

Clementine lunged at me, throwing out a shimmering pulse of magic. I slid under the counter as the spell exploded behind me, sending coffee cups and sugar packets flying.

"Don't make me go vamp on you. I have fangs, and I will use them." Sorcha was on top of the counter as spells flew around her. Vorana had wisely tucked herself at the back of the counter out of the spell blast range.

"Enough!" My magic wrapped around Clementine's wrist, locking it mid-spell. She gasped as the energy in her palm flickered out. For now, my magic was behaving, but I didn't know how long my luck would hold out, so I needed to move fast.

Zandra caught Emiline's next attack, twisting her spell in a counterspell and sending it spinning into the ceiling, where it burst into harmless light.

Emiline gritted her teeth. "You—"

I didn't let her finish. I leaped onto her shoulder, my tail wrapping around her neck like a magic dampener. Her power sputtered and died.

Emiline panted, fury in her eyes. "I suppose you want to kill us, too. Even after I helped you."

"That was never our plan." I hopped off Emiline's shoulder, landing lightly on the floor. "Now, if you're done wrecking the place, we can talk like adults and figure out what happened to Agatha."

Sorcha clambered off the counter, shaking her head as she looked at the mess.

"Let's leave them to it." Vorana gently tugged on Sorcha's arm.

Sorcha huffed out a breath. "We'll be in the kitchen. Don't break another thing or I'll start biting."

We waited until we had the place to ourselves before talking.

"We don't want to hurt you," Zandra said, as Emiline and Clementine glared at us with distrust. "But we need to find out what happened at the bar. We didn't murder Agatha."

"We saw you!" Emiline said.

"You're the eyewitnesses? What exactly did you see?" I asked.

"You yelled at Agatha." Clementine finally stopped struggling against my magical bindings.

"What were we yelling about?" I asked.

"Well, I'm not sure. But you yelled, and Agatha was upset." Emiline's eyes glazed for a second before they snapped back into focus.

"You don't sound too sure about that. Clementine," I asked, "what do you remember?"

"A fight, I think," Clementine said. "Everything got hazy and weird, and my head started spinning. I figured I had too much to drink."

"You both sound uncertain about what you witnessed," Zandra said.

"We're sure about one thing," Emiline said. "Our best friend is dead, and everyone's telling us you did it. And we saw you fighting. Who else would it be? We don't know anyone else in this town. And you had a grudge about your squashed tail."

"Our memory of last night is different," I said. "We partied with you and then left the bar around midnight. Agatha was still alive when we went home."

"The angels said that was when Agatha was killed," Clementine said. "Maybe you continued your fight outside, and we didn't see."

"Which means you didn't see us lay a finger on Agatha," I said. "You're only believing what the angels told you."

"I... I'm not sure. I'm certain I saw something. Why would the angels lie?" Clementine asked.

"Angel Force has been under stress," I said. "We can't rely on them."

"And you expect us to rely on you?" Emiline shook her head. "I thought we'd sorted everything after I healed your tail and there were no hard feelings about the limo. I guess not."

"We aren't that petty," I said. "And I was grateful you healed me. We need to know what happened to Agatha."

"We already know," Clementine said, although there was little conviction in her words.

"You have a hazy recollection of a fight that never happened," Zandra said. "Don't you see? Magic is involved. When we saw Agatha's body—"

"How have you seen her body?" Emiline interrupted. "We haven't been allowed to see her yet. Angel Force said they needed to conduct tests and an autopsy. After that, they'll release her body."

"That's not important," I said. "But Agatha got whacked with strange magic. You must have been too. Magic that led you to believe we murdered your best friend."

Emiline still didn't look convinced, although Clementine was wavering as she glanced at us and chewed on her bottom lip.

"We need to know about anyone who wanted to harm Agatha," I said. "What about friends, family, or a boyfriend?"

"You can count us out," Emiline said.

"Friends fall out," I said. "I often disagree with my closest friends. What's that saying? You always hurt the ones you love."

"Don't pin this murder on us. We have dozens of witnesses who saw us at the bar," Clementine said. "We were there all night."

"Not Agatha," I said. "Why did she go outside?"

"That's what she always does. She sneaks off, looking for adventure. All of us behaved normally last night. The odd ones out are you two."

"And yet you remember a fight that never happened," Zandra said.

Emiline and Clementine exchanged a glance.

"Could magic be messing with us? I do have a killer headache after last night," Emiline said. "I've felt nothing like it."

"That could be because of this weird magic," I said.

"You think someone came after us?" Clementine sounded hesitant.

"It's possible," I said. "Can you think of anyone who wanted Agatha dead? Maybe a family feud that followed her here?"

"She was only close to Thelma," Clementine said. "They haven't seen their parents for years. They had a falling out a long time ago and lost contact."

"Their parents are dead," Emiline said. "I saw their funeral notice about a year ago. It has nothing to do with them."

"What about a boyfriend?" Zandra asked.

"Yeah, and this will sound weird," Emiline said. "Agatha and Thelma were dating cousins. Billy and Freddie. The guys even look the same. It's sort of freaky when you see them together. Agatha and Thelma look so alike and so do their boyfriends."

"Was the relationship serious?" I asked.

"It depends who you talk to," Emiline said. "I don't think they were planning on getting married. Agatha enjoyed a good time and didn't want to get serious with anyone. She wasn't ready to settle down."

"Which was why she was looking for some fun with Remus and his hive," I said.

Emiline smiled tightly. "Agatha said it wasn't cheating if you fooled around with a vampire because he's dead. You can't cheat with the dead."

"Technically undead," I said.

"They both hated their jobs," Clementine said. "They work for a company that makes enchanted candles. Mrs. Wick: Traditional Charms and Enchantments."

"Yeah. It's the shift work they don't enjoy. They got stuck on evening shifts for the last month. They were talking about resigning but had found nothing they wanted to do. You could ask their boss if there were any problems, but I don't remember Agatha saying she had an issue with anyone she worked with."

"Let us have the details of Agatha's boyfriend and her employer. We'll check them out," I said.

"Give us a minute." Emiline tugged Clementine into a corner, and they whispered to each other before eventually nodding. They returned to join us.

"We're giving you the benefit of the doubt." Clementine wrote the information on a paper napkin. "Neither of us feels well, so maybe magic is messing with us. I know I heard a fight, but every time I focus on the details, it's like the memory has gone."

"Or been faked," I said.

Vorana hurried out of the kitchen and looked out the window at the front of the café. She dashed back. "We saw a troop of angels fly overhead when we were in the alley. Word must be spreading that you broke out."

"Broke out?" Emiline's worried gaze darted over us.

"There was a misunderstanding," I said. "It'll be cleared up by the end of today."

"Have you escaped from Angel Force?" Emiline slowly backed toward the door, taking Clementine with her. Her eyes narrowed. "You did it, didn't you? You killed Agatha. We're not misremembering. You're trying to find people to frame. We're not stupid. We saw what happened last night!"

Zandra held up her hands. "You didn't see a fight. We're sure there's weird magic at work. If you go around town, you'll see you're not the only ones affected. Vorana's bookstore even had people fighting in it yesterday, and nothing exciting ever happens in there."

"My bookstore is the most interesting place in this town." Vorana drew in a breath. "But my books have taken on a life of their own. I got knocked out last week when a hardback dinged me on the back of the head."

"And Sorcha's café is misbehaving," I added. "The freezer keeps getting covered in gross, sticky webbing that makes it malfunction. Someone is casting that magic."

"What's any of that got to do with you killing Agatha?" Clementine asked.

"There's something in Crimson Cove misdirecting magic," I said. "We don't know what it is, where it's coming from, or who's doing it, but we intend to stop it."

"I'm not buying this," Emiline said. "You're the only ones who are a danger to us. You killed Agatha, and you're confusing us by planting lies in our heads."

Before anyone could stop her, she yanked open the door and screamed at the top of her lungs. "Angels! They're down here. Stop Agatha's killers from getting away!"

Emiline was so loud, she caused a woman to shriek and jump so high she dropped her brown paper bag of groceries.

"Time to go." I dashed past Sorcha and Vorana, Zandra hot on my heels. "Did you get the details of Agatha's boyfriend and the work address?"

"Right here." Zandra waved the paper napkin.

"Let's start with the boyfriend before the angels take away our chance of freedom for good."

Chapter 7

Tricky magic

"That translocation spell felt like it was trying to tear my limbs off." Zandra shuddered as we landed in the quaintly named Ginger Drove, home to Agatha and Thelma's boyfriends, Billy and Freddie.

"It was risky to use it," I said, my fur still standing on end, a lingering aftereffect of the unwilling magic. "But we had to get here quickly. With Angel Force closing in, we're almost out of time."

I took in our surroundings. Ginger Drove was a typically pretty, small magical town. We'd landed by a weather-aged memorial listing magic users who'd fallen in the Battle of Greystone Heights.

It was lunchtime, and people were making their way home to eat or to grab a sandwich from the local store, not paying much attention to two strangers who'd just arrived.

We stopped a small, round witch with dark beady eyes, who pointed us to a bakery when we asked if she knew Billy and Freddie.

"If you're looking for somewhere good to eat, they've already shut," she said. "They open early, get out their orders to local businesses, and then serve until noon. Their tiger bread is well worth queuing for. They make delicious cherry tarts, too. And don't get me started on the croissants."

"Thank you for the suggestions, but we're not here for the treats," I said.

"If there are any treats, I'm always interested," Zandra said. "We've barely eaten today."

My stomach growled in agreement, but food would come later.

"They should still be at the bakery. You'll likely find them round the back, sorting the produce that hasn't been sold. They take it to those in need. They're good boys and always look out for others."

We thanked the witch for the information and followed her directions to the bakery, passing several cute, independent stores.

"Billy and Freddie aren't sounding like likely killers," Zandra said. "Two well-behaved guys who look after the less fortunate."

"Where love is involved, people are often unreasonable," I said. "It's easy for a fight to get out of hand, and before you know it, one of you is no longer breathing."

"That doesn't sound like love to me," Zandra said. "I'm surprised you say that. I'm the one who's usually cynical about relationships. Are things bad with you and Sammy?"

"As always, Sammy is divine light himself. I have no complaints. It's just that the more we see unkindness in people's hearts, the harder mine appears to become."

"Things really are off-kilter if you're having gloomy thoughts," Zandra said. "You always buck me up and tell me everything will be okay."

"And everything will be okay," I said. "Once we figure out the root cause of the troubles that ail Crimson Cove."

"Just a small job, then." Zandra's smile was wry. "Together, we'll fix things."

I looked up at her with surprise. She was right. Our roles had reversed. When had I gotten so cynical? It was the stress. Keeping secrets was never good for one's constitution.

"I like the look of this place." Zandra had slowed and stared at the delightful bakery with forest green trim. The display window showed a few chocolate croissants and a triple-layer carrot cake under a glass dome. The wooden counter was empty of treats, but a chalkboard menu listed delicious daily specials in neat handwriting. There was even the vague scent of warm bread lingering, no doubt aided by a touch of magic to entice shoppers in to buy an extra cake or goodie.

The sign on the door said closed, and when we tried the handle, it was locked. But there was an alleyway next to the building, which we walked along, and came to a door marked Staff Entrance. Zandra knocked, and we waited.

A couple of moments later, a man with twinkling green eyes and flour smeared on one cheek opened the door.

"Hey. If you're here for the goodwill donations, it'll be another ten minutes," he said. "We had a last-minute rush because Billy made a batch of his triple chocolate and cherry brownies, so we got behind. Although... you're not our usual person. Are you goodwill or not?"

"We're not," I said, "but it sounds like a worthy cause. Are you Freddie or Billy?"

He tilted his head. "I'm Freddie Carson. If you're not from the food bank, then..."

"Greetings, I'm Juno, and this is my wonderful witch, Zandra Crypt. Do you have a few minutes to spare?"

Freddie glanced over his shoulder. "Not really. What's this about?"

"Agatha Black," Zandra said. "We're involved with Angel Force in Crimson Cove."

"Oh. Right. Have you been trying to get through to us this morning?"

"Most likely," I bluffed.

"We've been so slammed in the bakery that we've not had five minutes to ourselves." Freddie gestured us inside. "I just checked the messages and saw two from a number I didn't recognize. Was that you?"

"That's why we're here." I gently smoothed over the mild deception to avoid Freddie growing suspicious. Angel Force must have been in touch to let them know about Agatha's death.

"Is everything okay with Agatha?" Freddie asked.

"Perhaps we could talk inside?" I suggested.

"Um... yeah. Sure. Come through. Billy is in the kitchen, bagging the food." Freddie's expression had morphed from jovial to serious, as if he sensed bad news was coming his way, which it often did when Angel Force got involved in your life.

A man with the same remarkable good looks and twinkling eyes was in the kitchen, a stack of bread beside him. He looked up when we entered. "Who's this?"

"They're from Angel Force," Freddie said. "This is my cousin, Billy. He's dating Agatha. Thelma is my girl."

"It's good to meet you," I said. "And I'm sorry to say we come with bad news."

"Not bad news about Agatha?" Billy set down the sliced loaf he held.

"There's no easy way to put this. There was an incident, and Agatha was involved."

"Which bones has she broken this time?" Freddie asked. "She's always the crazy one. She drives Thelma mad, but she's impossible to control."

"It's a little more serious than that," I said. "Agatha was found dead in Crimson Cove."

Billy's body jerked, and he staggered to a stool by the table, leaning on it. "I don't understand. You said there'd been an incident. Death is more than an incident."

"We're still figuring out what happened," I said, "which is why we're here."

Freddie looked almost as shocked as Billy. He hurried over and clasped his cousin's shoulder. "What else can you tell us?"

"Agatha, Thelma, and their friends were in Crimson Cove for a vacation," I said cautiously, aware the men most likely didn't know the girls planned on visiting Remus's vampire hive for a specific kind of fun.

Freddie nodded. "They told us about that. They often have these ladies' weekends—that's what they like to call them. Have drinks, fancy meals, get massages. Honestly, it sounds like fun, but they always say no boys are allowed. I figured it was their way of blowing off steam."

"We met them when they arrived in Crimson Cove," I said. "The limousine they hired had broken down."

"Limousine!" Freddie's eyebrows rose. "I guess they really were out to have a good time." He looked at Billy, who remained silent, staring into space. "What else can you tell us about what happened to Agatha?"

"We're running tests, and there'll be an autopsy, but the initial findings suggest magic killed her. We don't know what kind yet, and we don't know who cast the spell," Zandra said.

"I... I was going to ask her to marry me," Billy whispered. "I adored Agatha. She was the only one for me."

That was a different story from the one Clementine and Emiline had told.

"I'm so sorry for your loss," I said. "Agatha seemed like fun."

"She was the life and soul of any party," Freddie said when Billy didn't answer. "I'm not sure she was ready to settle for marriage, though."

"I was. I only wanted her," Billy said. "Are you sure you haven't made a mistake?"

"We've confirmed it was Agatha," Zandra said. "We want to know more about her background to fill in the missing pieces of her life."

"So you can find out who did this to her?" Freddie asked. "Was it someone from Crimson Cove she annoyed?"

"Agatha didn't annoy people," Billy said.

"Buddy, I know you were into her, but Agatha wasn't everyone's cup of triple roast organic latte. She could be over the top. I was used to it, but not everyone was so tolerant. I prefer Thelma's more laid-back approach. She's the sensible sister."

"Agatha could be sensible!"

"Not wanting to speak ill of the departed, but name one time when she's been sensible?" Freddie asked.

"I... I'll think of something." Billy stared into space again, pale with shock.

"When did this happen?" Freddie asked.

"Late last night, around midnight," I said. "And I'm sorry to ask this, but could you tell us where you both were at that time?"

"It wasn't me!" Billy stood upright and whacked a hand on the table. "I adored that woman. I wanted to marry her!"

"Easy now. They're just doing their job," Freddie said. "They have to ask these questions. We want to know what happened, don't we? Sorry about Billy."

"It's fine," I said. "This news has been a shock."

"I can answer for both of us," Freddie said. "We live together. Last night was a big rugby tournament, so we stayed up late to watch the match. Our team won, so we celebrated."

"Was it just the two of you celebrating?" Zandra asked.

Freddie nodded. "Just us. We do most things together. Watch sports. Run a business. Date sisters. It works. We didn't leave the house all evening. We finished at the bakery around three, did our food boxing as usual, grabbed an early dinner, and then watched the game."

Billy stirred to life. "You must find out what happened to Agatha. I don't know what I'll do without her."

Freddie mumbled soft words to his cousin. "How's Thelma taking it? We're not as serious as Billy was with Agatha, but I'm still worried about her."

"She's naturally upset," I said.

"What about suspects? Do you have any?" Freddie asked.

I kept my expression neutral. "Certain individuals are being looked into, but we're certain there are more suspects to be discovered."

"I hope they never see the light of day again," Billy said. "Agatha was my everything. It's wrong for someone to take that away."

"We'll get whoever did this," Zandra said. "You can guarantee that."

"Did Agatha mention any problems at work?" I asked.

"She said it was boring," Freddie said. "She worked at the enchanted candle place with Thelma. It was shift work, which wasn't great for our social life. They often got called in at the last minute because someone was off sick or hadn't shown up for their shift. They always went in because they needed extra money for their trips away. They didn't love it. It was just work. It got them the money to do the things they liked."

"Isn't that what most people do a job for?" Zandra asked.

"Not us," Freddie said proudly, looking around the kitchen with a fond expression. "We love baking. It's in our blood. Our family has owned this bakery for five hundred years."

"Not everyone is as lucky as we are," Billy said. "We get to do a job that's our passion. It makes it feel as if you never work a day in your life when you achieve that."

"How fortunate," I said.

"Is that how you feel working for Angel Force?" Freddie asked.

"We do this on a consultancy basis," I said. "Stopping injustices gives us satisfaction. But we also work at animal control."

Freddie's bottom lip jutted out. "Huh! That's an unusual career mix."

"It makes life interesting."

"What happens next?" Billy asked.

"We keep talking to people who knew Agatha and put together a detailed understanding of her life," I said. "It'll help us find out if she had problems with anyone."

"What about her relationship with Thelma?" Zandra asked.

"They were tight. They did everything together," Freddie said. "It was kinda cute but also frustrating, if you know what I mean. It was almost impossible to get any alone time with Thelma."

Billy nodded. "They lived together, just like us. People make fun of us because sisters are dating two cousins and our lives are so similar, but we don't care. We're happy. Well, we were until you showed up with this terrible news. Man, I can't believe it. Agatha isn't coming home."

Freddie comforted Billy by plating a brownie and setting it in front of him. Zandra's stomach growled, but she didn't ask for a brownie of her own.

"What about any problems between Agatha and Clementine or Emiline?" I asked.

"There was nothing," Freddie said. "That group of girls got on well. Of course, they had the occasional squabble, but they've been friends since they were kids and always hung out together. They were talking about getting a bigger place, so Clementine and Emiline could move in."

"I can't see any problem between them big enough to kill over," Billy said. "It wasn't any of them. And we had nothing to do with it. It must have been someone in Crimson Cove. Is it a safe town? Agatha would never upset anyone, so you're looking for an unstable person. Start with the lowlifes. Local criminals. What about gangs? Do you have gangs in that town?"

Freddie raised his eyebrows at us but said nothing, realizing Billy's grief was making him ramble.

"Crimson Cove is a delightful town," I said. "We moved there because we liked it so much.

We always monitor troublemakers and send them packing."

Billy grunted, not looking convinced. "You must have missed someone."

"We're exploring all possibilities," I said. "Is Mrs. Wick's candle factory close by?"

"Oh. Sure. It's a twenty-minute walk from here," Freddie said. "It runs around the clock, so you'll find someone there at all hours. Turn right when you head out of the bakery and keep going straight. It's the huge cream building in front of you. You can't miss it. It has a turret shaped like a sparkling candle."

"You're wasting your time going there," Billy said. "Neither Agatha nor Thelma enjoyed their job, but they had no problems with the people there. They didn't even mind Mrs. Wick, and not everyone can say they like their boss. You need to go back to Crimson Cove. That's where the trouble is."

"We appreciate the input, but we must cover all bases," I said. "Thank you for your time. And once again, I'm sorry for your loss."

Freddie showed us out, issuing a soft apology for Billy's rambling before shutting the door behind us.

We walked to the end of the alley in silence and began our journey towards Mrs. Wick's factory.

"What did you think of those two?" Zandra asked.

"The news genuinely shocked Billy."

"So much so, he didn't even eat that brownie. Did you see the size of it?" Zandra's stomach growled again.

I chuckled. "I did. Billy has a rose-tinted view of Agatha. Unlike Freddie. I got the impression Freddie found her annoying."

"Annoying enough to sneak to Crimson Cove and murder her while she's on a fun night out?"

"Most likely not. But Billy had a different view of their relationship," I said. "If Agatha wasn't serious about him, but he was into her, he could have felt rejected. Maybe he got Freddie to cover for him while he headed to Crimson Cove and killed her."

Zandra didn't look convinced, and neither was I. Billy had been stunned by the news of Agatha's murder.

"It's just a theory," I added. "We should message Sage. She can ask around and find out if Billy or Freddie were seen near Crimson Cove when Agatha was murdered."

A warm swoosh of air ruffled my fur, and I looked up to see Finn swooping down. He landed superhero-style on the ground and shook out his wings before fixing us with a cold smile.

"What are you doing here?" I asked. "Do you have leads for us to follow?"

"No leads. But you need to scram." Finn stalked toward us.

"There's a problem?" Zandra asked.

"Cythera is hot on your heels. I can run interference to buy you time, but when she finds you here, there'll be no getting away. If you value your freedom, get moving."

Chapter 8

Hidden trouble

I hunched beside Zandra, not amused the rain had started as soon as we'd returned to Crimson Cove. We were tucked deep in the woods as night fell, and I'd risked using a cover spell to ensure the angels wouldn't find us.

Finn had told us the best place to be was the last place Angel Force would look, and that was home. There was logic to that thought train, and since Cythera had brought a troop of angels to Ginger Drove to look for us, we heeded his advice.

"I hate being out here," Zandra murmured, leaning back against a damp tree trunk. "I keep getting the feeling I'm being watched."

I'd sensed it, too. There was a spiky feel to the magic, and my hackles had lifted not long after we'd concealed ourselves. But I didn't want to worry my witch when she was already stressed. "There are all sorts of critters living in these woods. It's why we advise people to stay clear of them late at night."

"What's worse? Angry angels wanting to charge us with murder or enchanted creatures wanting to take a bite out of us?" Zandra asked.

"At least we're used to the biting critters," I said.

"And the angry angels." Zandra smirked, flicking up the collar on her jacket and hunching over, trying to stay warm. "We've found ourselves in some messes, but this has got to be the biggest yet. We've always been able to talk ourselves out of anything with Cythera. It doesn't feel like we'll do that this time."

"We will. We can get ourselves out of any mess," I said. "Nothing is too big that we can't defeat it if we work together."

Zandra jumped and spun around. "I'm sure something is watching us. I keep getting this creeping feeling running up and down my spine."

"We're uneasy because Angel Force wants to bring us in and keep us behind bars," I said. "I see nothing, and my eyesight is superior to yours."

"My vision is great. They're hiding, and they're good at it." Zandra lifted her hand and sparked a light ball. It glowed for a few seconds before sputtering out with a disgruntled hiss.

"And the magic is going wrong again now we're back in Crimson Cove." Zandra sighed. "Maybe it was safer to stay behind bars."

"Not the way Cythera is behaving," I said. "She's got it in for us. Until we get her to see sense, we can't risk being around her."

"At least we have Finn on our side."

"I'm not so sure we do. He's not taking this seriously. Finn just wants to cause chaos and mess with his boss. He doesn't care about us. Not when his demon is troubling him." I peered intently into the gloom, watching for any flash of movement. "What about asking for Bertoli's help? He can be uptight, but he's mellowed, and he's helped in the past."

"He helps grudgingly. He'll be too scared of Cythera to go against her," Zandra said. "Even if Bertoli thinks we're innocent, if she tells him to charge us, he'll do it."

"Bertoli is on the side of justice, just like us," I said.

"I'm not taking that risk," Zandra said. "We need to make a better plan. One with no dubious angels."

Before she could utter another word, a weird wave of magic whacked into us. It sent Zandra sprawling onto her back and caused my fur to stand on end, as if I got smacked with an electrical charge.

A man appeared, crouched over with his head down and his arms wrapped around his knees.

I inhaled deeply. I recognized his scent. It was Zandra's father! Abel looked green and took a moment to retch violently.

"Dad! What are you doing here?" Zandra scrambled to her feet and stared in disbelief at her father.

He held up a hand as he finished his retching. "Sorry, I don't handle powerful magic well, and I didn't cast that spell. Jeez! I'm lucky to be in one piece."

Zandra hurried over and helped him to his feet. He pulled out a mint and stuck it into his mouth before smiling at her. "It's good to see you, kiddo. Sorry for the dramatic entrance."

Zandra hugged him. "I'm happy to see you, too, but I'm still shocked. Who sent you?"

"Granny Dottie. Although it took half a dozen attempts to get the translocation spell working. The first two times she tried, I got sent somewhere completely different, and she had to drag me back. Not fun. Especially when she's in such a foul mood."

"No wonder you're feeling so unwell," I said. "Is Granny Dottie having trouble with her powers?"

"Not just her. That's why I'm here. There's trouble with all the Crypt witches. Something bad is happening in Willow Tree Falls. The witches are misfiring, and the demon prison is vulnerable. They sent me here because I'm the least valuable member of the family when looking after the demons."

"That's not true," I said.

Abel shrugged. "I know my place with those incredible witches, and it's not as their alpha. That suits me."

"What's going on back home?" Zandra asked.

"There have been minor glitches for a while. You know about the prison breakouts?"

"Sure. I was there at the last big one," Zandra said. "But I thought everything was under control. When I left to come back here, everything felt stable."

"And it was, but only for a short time. It wasn't long before we found new breaches in the barriers and demons creeping out. Everyone's working around the clock to hold things together, but they're only patching the problem. They can't find its source."

"That sounds worryingly familiar," I said.

"Maybe we should go to Willow Tree Falls. We need somewhere safe to stay," Zandra said.

"Safe? What's going on here that makes it unsafe?" Abel asked. "Does it have something to do with you hiding in a forest at night?"

"It does. Angel Force believes we murdered a witch," I said. "We had to escape incarceration to clear our names. We need to keep a low profile until we figure things out."

Abel's mouth dropped open. "You'd never do that!"

"Escape a prison cell or murder a witch?"

"Both. Either." He shook his head. "You're innocent."

"We know, but the angels won't accept that," Zandra said. "And they won't listen to reason."

"Why do they think you're involved?" Abel asked.

"There are witnesses who say we did it. Fingers are being pointed toward us, and we've yet to find a decent suspect to present as an alternative," I said.

His forehead furrowed. "Is someone targeting the Crypt witches? Tempest's behavior is still not right after she was framed for murdering that tech mage."

"This is the first I've heard about that," Zandra said. "Why didn't you tell me Tempest was struggling?"

"Your mother didn't want you to worry." Abel squeezed her shoulder. "But it's more than that. The demon prison has been unstable on and off for months. And now this! Angel Force believes you killed someone."

"This family gathers enemies," I said. "No demon is a friend to the Crypt witches. Could it be your past returning to wreak revenge?"

"We've faced down enemies before, but this feels different," Abel said. "I know you're innocent. I'll help any way I can."

"Perhaps a trip to Willow Tree Falls would be wise," I said. "We'll have space to think."

"I'm not so sure you should visit. It's dangerous. That was one reason Granny Dottie sent me away. You can all protect yourselves, whereas my magic is average at best. I don't want to get in the way and risk anyone's life."

"Crimson Cove is no better," Zandra said. "We're having the same magic glitches, and we have a troop of angry angels on our tail. At least we can help in Willow Tree Falls. At the moment, we're hiding and getting frustrated with our lack of progress."

"Let me get in touch with the family. I'll see what they suggest. We could use the help in Willow Tree Falls, even though the others won't like to admit that." Abel hesitated. "Won't it be a risk for you to go there, though? Angel Force will be on the lookout for you, and they'll assume you'll seek refuge with your family."

"We need to be there," Zandra said. "I don't want any of you at risk. We can help."

I nodded. "We should. If we lose control of the demon prison, we'll have much bigger issues than a murder charge to deal with."

"I'll see what they say. If Granny Dottie gives me the green light, we should head back there now," Abel said.

"Before we do," I said, "we need more information on our victim. We were planning to visit her employer, but the angels blocked our access. They should have cleared out by now, so we'll do that then join you in Willow Tree Falls."

Abel hugged Zandra. "That'll give me time to convince your mom we need to be together. She's so concerned about others getting hurt. Stay safe. I'll do whatever I can to protect you. I'll go into town and see what the latest news is."

"Thanks, Dad. Stay alert when you're in town. There is all kinds of weird going on, and I don't want you getting messed up in it."

"And look out for Angel Force too," I said. "If they see you in town, they'll assume you're here to help us, and we don't want you getting caught up in our mess."

"That's what parents are for," Abel said. "Shall I meet you back here in an hour?"

"That will give us enough time," I said.

Abel headed off through the trees toward town.

Zandra kicked her booted foot through the damp earth. "I must help my family, but I'll be no good to them if the angels catch us before we've cleared our names."

"Then let's hope whoever is behind this murder reveals themselves as guilty so we can solve this and focus on what's important."

"If only it were that easy." Zandra slowly surveyed the dripping trees.

"We should be okay to return to Ginger Drove. By now, the angels will have finished their search and convinced themselves we're not there. And with

Finn running misdirection, we've got extra time," I said.

"That's assuming he did what he said he would. We can't rely on anybody," Zandra said. "Do you want to risk a translocation spell? It's the quickest way to get there, although it may not be the safest if the magic goes hinky."

"I'll cast. My magic has been behaving." With effort and only a slight misfire that felt like the magic wanted to flay me alive, I got us to Ginger Drove. We landed a short distance from Mrs. Wick's factory with its impressive candle-shaped sparkling turret.

After checking around to ensure no angels were lurking, we dashed to the factory door and headed inside and through the empty reception area.

The factory floor was bustling, and bright overhead lights made it impossible to hide anywhere. There was an open-plan work area with twenty staff members boxing candles and casting spells over them.

We checked with a staff member and discovered Mrs. Wick had an office on the floor above.

We headed upstairs and found her at her desk. She was a sleek woman with iron-gray hair, wearing a long black dress printed with candles. When we arrived, she was peering at a pile of paperwork.

"Greetings," I said. "I hope we're not interrupting."

Her head whipped up, and her eyes narrowed. "Am I expecting you?"

"No, but we were in the area and hoped you could answer some questions." I made the introductions, placing heavy emphasis on our expert consultant role with Angel Force to get her attention.

"I don't know how I can help you any more than I already have," Mrs. Wick said.

"You already know about Agatha?" Zandra asked.

"Of course. Don't you lot talk to each other? I received a message earlier today."

"That would have been our liaison team," I said. "Was it Cythera?"

"No. An angel called Finn. He wasn't friendly, but then I suppose dealing with death will never cheer a person up."

"Finn! That's right. He's been so busy, he must have forgotten to pass on the update to us. We wanted to speak in more detail with everyone close to Agatha," I said.

"Then you don't need to talk to me," Mrs. Wick said. "Excuse me a moment. I must check the last order of the day is going out on time. If I give my team an inch, they forget to load the last boxes, and then I'm left to make the final deliveries myself. Take a seat. I won't be long. Don't touch the candles! They're enchanted." Mrs. Wick bustled out of the room, and we looked around, taking in the attractive, candle-themed decor. Candles were on every surface in all shapes, sizes, and colors.

"This woman loves her candles," Zandra said. "They have their uses when casting spells, but I find the scented ones give me a headache."

"They don't do my booping snooter much good either," I said.

"Sorry about that. Everything's fixed now," Mrs. Wick said, returning to her seat. "What do you need to know about Agatha?"

"How long did she work for you?" I asked.

"Two years. She used to work in the service industry but didn't enjoy it and wanted to do something more hands-on with magic. I suppose this was a reasonable fit, although the enchantments cast on the candles are the regular variety, so it's not exciting work. But there's always a demand for our products, so she was kept busy. Idle hands and all that."

"Could you describe your relationship with Agatha?" I asked.

"It was an employer-employee relationship. I wouldn't say we were friends, but we rubbed along well enough. I like to keep things professional. No fraternizing with the staff. It only blurs boundaries."

"Agatha never got in any trouble or was written up?" Zandra asked.

"I had to reprimand her because her timekeeping was poor. Thelma did her best to get Agatha here when she was supposed to be. It worked best when I paired their shifts, so they always worked together. Thelma would chivvy Agatha along."

"Did it annoy you that Agatha was unreliable?" I asked.

"She's not the first member of my team who thinks timekeeping isn't important," Mrs. Wick said. "I highly value it. I think if you're five minutes early, you're on time, and if you're on time, you're five minutes late. Live by those rules, you never leave the other person waiting and have wiggle room should something unexpected appear and divert you."

"I couldn't agree more," I said. "When a person is late, it suggests they don't value your time."

"Exactly! I said that to Agatha once, and she thought it was amusing. She found a lot of things funny. She lived from moment to moment, enjoying herself, I suppose. If you can have that mindset, it's all well and good, but when you run a business, you must make plans, or everything fails. I have a big workforce here, so I can't afford to be sloppy."

"Did you consider Agatha's working methods sloppy?" I asked.

"No, but she needed watching. Once she learned how to do things and got into a routine, she was fine, but I never put her on the very last shift because she'd be eager to go home and would make excuses."

"It sounds like she was a difficult employee," Zandra said.

"She really wasn't. I could tell you a few stories about what my employees get up to, but now is not the time. I had no problems with her, and I'm sorry she's dead." Mrs. Wick lifted her coffee mug then realized it was empty and set it down with a disgruntled huff. "Do you know what happened to her? The angel I spoke to was vague."

"That's what we're investigating," Zandra said. "We need to find out why someone wanted her dead."

"Well, I'm not sure what else I can tell you," Mrs. Wick said. "Like I said, Agatha did her job to a reasonable standard, and I had no issue with her.

We weren't close, and she didn't confide in me. It was always the sisters together. Agatha and Thelma did everything together. They looked out for each other."

"Would you mind telling us where you were on the night of Agatha's murder?" I asked.

"I can tell you again, just like I did your colleague, but it hasn't changed from the last time," Mrs. Wick said. "Your team needs to coordinate better."

"We're working on it. Angel Force is such a large organization that information slips through the cracks," I said. "Just remind us if you'd be so kind."

"I was here. The factory operates all hours of the day and night. We're the sole distributor for all schools and academies within a five-hundred-mile radius."

"You worked a late shift?" I asked.

"I was here until one in the morning. I'd had several members of staff call in unwell. There's a strain of pink eye going around, and it's terribly contagious. I did my paperwork then rolled up my sleeves and got stuck in on the factory floor. It was fun. It's been a while since I've done the hands-on work. That's how this factory started. Just me in my spare bedroom, enchanting candles. That was ten years ago."

"You've grown quite an empire," Zandra said.

"I like to keep busy." Mrs. Wick glanced over my head and stiffened. "I am sorry, but I have things to do. If you have no further questions, I must get on."

"Thanks for your time," I said. "We may be in touch again."

She nodded a goodbye as we left her office and headed down the stairs and through the factory, dodging the busy workers.

"I couldn't find a motive there," I said. "If Mrs. Wick was here at the time of the murder, then she's got an alibi."

"Let's check before we go," Zandra said.

We spent ten minutes talking to some of the factory staff, and sure enough, Mrs. Wick had been on the factory floor that night. She was innocent.

We reached the exit at the back of the factory, and I looked over my shoulder. Mrs. Wick stood in her office door, her arms folded over her chest, and a pensive look on her face.

"On to the next suspect." Zandra pushed open the door, and we found ourselves confronted by a troop of angels.

Chapter 9

Trapped

I looked back again at Mrs. Wick. She was swiftly shutting her door. I growled softly. She'd contacted Angel Force to let them know we were visiting and asking questions. They must have alerted her to watch out for us.

Cythera was among the group of angels preventing our escape. Her eyes blazed with fury as she stepped forward. "I knew you couldn't be trusted."

"You must understand why we escaped," I replied, my gaze shifting over the angel troop to see what we were up against. "We have to clear our names."

"You've made the situation worse," Cythera said. "You planned on clearing up loose ends to make us believe you're innocent. You've been hiding evidence of your crimes."

"We are innocent!" Zandra stood beside me with her hands fisted. "Other than some witnesses you allege to have, you've got no evidence that we had anything to do with what happened to

Agatha. That's why we're here. Trying to find actual suspects and stopping you from making the biggest mistake in your already less than glowing career."

"You're unnaturally strong magic users," Cythera said. "It's well within your power to end another's life."

"As it is yours," I said. "But you use your powers for good. As do we."

I'd noticed Finn was missing from the group of angels. A wiggle of worry settled in my stomach. Had Cythera figured out he'd helped us escape our cell and distract the angels while they searched for us?

"If you're looking for your insider spy, he's off the case," Cythera said, her lip curling in disgust. "Finn isn't trustworthy if he's prepared to help the likes of you."

"He helped us because he knows you're wrong," I said. "He believes we're innocent."

"Finn is a muddled mix of demon and angel. We should never have allowed him to join Angel Force," Cythera said. "At least that's one issue remedied."

"You fired Finn?" I blinked in surprise.

"Suspended for now, but it's only a matter of time before I get rid of him for good," Cythera said. "Your loyal followers are fading away, and soon you'll be powerless."

"You make us sound like we're cult leaders," Zandra said. "All we've ever done is help Angel Force, and this is how you repay us?"

Cythera stamped her foot, and her wings flared wide. "I know everything. Tell me why you did it."

"We have no reason to want Agatha dead," I said.

Cythera's expression darkened. "More lies. Something happened between you and those witches. Something you considered so unforgivable you had to end their lives."

"Their lives?" I asked. "Is someone else dead?"

"Yes. And you know what happened because you did it." Cythera's voice rang with accusation, sending a chill down my spine.

"We've been too busy clearing our names to eat, let alone commit murder." There was a faint wobble in Zandra's voice. She sensed how much trouble we were in.

"If you're accusing us of a second murder, at least give us a name," I said.

"We discovered Thelma Black dead two hours ago." Cythera stepped closer, her wings casting a shadow over me. "Is that another coincidence? You escape from custody and Agatha's sister dies?"

The air left my lungs as if someone had punched me in the gut. Thelma was dead, too? My mind scrambled for an explanation, but all I could hear was the deafening rush of blood in my ears.

Cythera's lips curled into a triumphant sneer. "Your luck has run out. As soon as I discovered you'd escaped, I sent word to everyone you might contact. I warned them to be careful if you showed up."

"Which is why Mrs. Wick told you we were here," I said. "She hid her worries about us well. Does she know what happened to Thelma?"

"We've kept that out of the public sphere for now. We'll get the truth out of you, though."

Zandra lifted her chin. "We're happy to tell you how innocent we are. What happened to Thelma?"

Cythera crossed her arms. "You murdered her after chasing and terrifying her."

"That's not what happened! We visited Thelma to find out what she knew about Agatha's death," I protested, but Cythera wasn't listening.

"Thelma was vulnerable, broken, and you sought her out and destroyed her because you knew she'd testify to your guilt." Venom laced Cythera's voice. "I don't know why yet, but I will find out why you murdered those witches."

I forced my voice to remain steady. "It's true. We visited Thelma, but we didn't harm her."

"Witnesses say otherwise," Cythera snapped. "People heard her scream for help. And then the two of you were seen fleeing the crime scene."

"Thelma died right after we spoke to her?" Zandra asked.

"The magic used to destroy her was the same dark force used on Agatha." Cythera leaned in. "All I need to do is trace that magic back to you and your freedom will be taken away for good."

"The killer must have seen us leaving the rental and realized it was an opportunity to frame us for another crime," I said. "When we left that house, Thelma was alive. Screaming for help, but alive."

Cythera let out a sharp, humorless laugh. "Stop your lies. I'm done with them. You've always considered me foolish, unimportant. You belittle Angel Force and act like you're superior to everyone else."

"I don't act. I know my worth."

The air crackled. Cythera's wings shifted, and her hands clenched. Under any other circumstance, I might have thrown out another witty remark, but my pulse hammered in my throat. This wasn't just an accusation. Cythera wanted to prove we were guilty of two murders. If she achieved her ambition, freedom would become a distant memory. And there was no way I was letting my wonderful, innocent witch get stuck behind bars for the rest of her life.

"Have you found nothing suspicious when questioning other suspects?" I asked, trying to pull Cythera away from this unnatural and incorrect obsession over our guilt.

"We've spoken to Agatha and Thelma's boyfriends," Zandra said. "Billy and Freddie alibi for each other. It could be a cover."

"More likely, you intimidated them to get them to admit guilt," Cythera shot back. "Did you threaten their lives? Tell them to implicate themselves to allow you to get away?"

"That's ridiculous," I said. "And they'd never do it. Why would they?"

"Desperate criminals have no boundaries." Cythera took a deep breath then exhaled. "You failed. This is the end of the line for both of you. I'm taking you back into custody, and we'll be charging you with double murder."

I leaned against Zandra's leg, grounding myself. "That's not happening. You have no evidence against us."

Cythera's mouth twisted into a smirk. "Then I'll invent some."

A chill ran down my spine. Cythera wasn't stopping until we were locked away, or worse.

"I'm done with the two of you," she said. "Crimson Cove will be a better, safer, quieter place once you're behind bars. Angels, round them up."

The moment they moved, I jumped onto Zandra's shoulder. "You run. I'll distract them."

"There's no way I'm abandoning you. If we're fighting, we fight together."

I dabbed my booping snooter on her cheek. "Then we fight for freedom." With claws extended, my magic sparking like fire along my fur. I leaped, twisting midair, summoning a pulse of energy that exploded outward. The nearest angel stumbled back, wings flaring as the blast sent him skidding across the ground.

Zandra hurled a wave of shimmering blue energy, forcing two more angels to shield themselves as the spell ricocheted off their wings.

Cythera growled. "You're only making this worse!"

"Worse than false imprisonment? I doubt that." I landed on my paws and darted toward another angel.

She tried to snatch me, but I was faster. I sank my claws into her leg and channeled a jolt of magic through her. She yelped, her wings snapping outward as light crackled around her in defense.

Before I could strike again, something slammed into me. Pain exploded through my ribs as a force yanked me back like an invisible chain. It was a golden net. Cythera's doing. She flung me toward the ground, the net tightening like molten steel.

"Juno!" Zandra shouted.

I writhed, snarling, my fur standing on end. Magic burned against my skin, the net designed to suppress my power, and it was working. I had to tear through it so I could keep fighting.

Zandra's fury was instant when she saw I wasn't getting free. She slashed her hand through the air, summoning a wall of shadow between us and the angels.

One angel countered with a bolt of pure light piercing through the shadows. Another sent a shockwave of energy rippling across the ground, knocking Zandra off her feet.

She hit the ground hard and didn't get up.

Cythera advanced, glowing bindings forming in her hands. "Enough of this. The more you fight, the guiltier you seem."

Zandra tried to rise, but an angel pinned her, shackling her wrists with glowing cuffs. She thrashed, magic sparking at her fingertips, but the cuffs dimmed it instantly. A suppression spell.

I struggled harder, twisting, biting at the net, but Cythera was ready. She flicked her fingers, and the net constricted, pressing the air from my lungs. I let out a ragged snarl but couldn't break free.

Cythera loomed over me. "You're finished, Juno. It's over."

Zandra's frantic gaze locked onto mine. I wanted to tell her we'd find a way out of this. That we'd fight. We'd win. But a cold snap of magic around us sealed our fate. We were overwhelmed.

The angels hoisted Zandra to her feet, her hands bound. Another lifted me, the net tightening, cutting into my fur.

We were captured. Defeated.

Cythera exhaled, her victory obvious. "Take them in. Be careful. They're devious. Don't let them fool you."

And just like that, we were dragged away, about to be charged with crimes we didn't commit.

How were we getting out of this?

Chapter 10

Frozen toe beans

"I'm sure the angels have made this cell colder than it needs to be. It's to punish us for fighting them." I snuggled against Zandra, my eyes shut and my tail thrashing.

After we'd given in to Angel Force and allowed them to take us back to Crimson Cove, Cythera had whisked us through processing in record time and stuck us in the cell we'd escaped out of. She tripled the magic wards around it and ordered an angel to stand guard at all times. She was determined we wouldn't get away again.

Zandra had her back against the wall and her gaze on the ceiling. "I don't blame them for being angry. We didn't come quietly. Maybe it would have been better if we had."

I looked up at her. "You sound defeated."

"We are defeated! Angel Force has us, and they have witnesses to say we committed two murders."

"We can't give up. Not now. We're not the only ones in trouble. Your family needs help."

Zandra sighed. "I haven't forgotten. That's what I've been thinking about all night. Dad will be wondering what happened to us. He must have come here and found out we'd been captured."

"I expect the angels are denying us visitors as another form of punishment. They'll try to block legal help, too."

"They can't deny us that if this situation gets that bad," Zandra said. "He'll be worried. We should have gone with him when we had the chance. Instead, we had to be the heroes and solve the crime. It got us nowhere, and I'm now powerless to help my family when they need me."

"They're made of potent stuff. They'll figure out what to do with their demon problem, even if we can't assist right now."

"Not if everybody's magic is misfiring," Zandra said. "What if Dad's right? There could be someone going after the family. They tried to take Tempest down by framing her for Erick Farten's murder. They even wrote her name in the dirt. And she *was* acting strangely. She's always been snappy, but that was a new level of snark and disinterest. It wasn't her. She was under the influence of something, but I didn't pay the problem enough attention."

"Once the murder was solved and Tempest could go home, she seemed better. It could have just been stress making her act up." Even as I spoke, I didn't believe my own words. Tempest's magic was off-kilter. I'd felt intensely uneasy around her. She was famous for being prickly, but never toward Zandra. She'd taken her under her wing and trained her in all forms of Crypt witch magic. That was how they'd bonded. Sure, they fought, just like all siblings, but there was that intense bond of sisterhood that kept them together.

If some form of insidious magic had affected Tempest, it would be strong enough to affect the rest of the Crypt witches. And if they all fell, it wouldn't just be Willow Tree Falls in peril.

That was why we needed to get out and make the angels see sense.

"Cythera is looking at the detail when she should look at the bigger picture," I said. "It's what we keep circling but can't get a grip on. It's not just these isolated crimes that should be focused on, but how it all fits together."

"It's the town's wonky magic. We've talked about it," Zandra said. "Crimson Cove has always been spicy, but this level of magical spice is too hot for me to handle."

"I wish I'd spoken to Randal about inspecting the ley lines," I said. "He can always spot when something is out of alignment and work out a solution."

"Yeah, well, we're not dealing with him," Zandra said. "He won't be in town for much longer, so he won't care about our problems."

"He'll always care. And I know he'll always be fond of you," I said. "But he's admitted defeat. You held him at arm's length for too long, so he's moving on."

Zandra tensed. "You're saying that our failed relationship was all my fault?"

"No! I understand your caution about getting into a relationship. And Randal, well, he's his own worst enemy. Being backward in coming forward."

"We tried dating, and it was a flop. Randal is getting out of Crimson Cove, and good luck to him. We should have done the same when we had the chance. Then we wouldn't be stuck in a cell, accused of these crimes." Zandra thumped her head back against the wall.

I'd wondered a time or two about leaving Crimson Cove, but I couldn't imagine leaving our friends and found family. Not being able to drop into Vorana's bookstore whenever we liked or overindulge on Sorcha's delicious treats in the café. It felt wrong to vanish when times were tough.

"We need to figure out when the problems started," I said. "Was the attempt to frame Tempest the first incident, or did things begin before that?"

"We can puzzle over it all we like," Zandra said, "but while we're in here, we're as good as useless. Magical blunts with no power to do anything."

I ignored my witch's glum tone. "We need to get Cythera to look at other cases and make the connection."

"She won't! She thinks it's us, and that's all she cares about," Zandra said. "And she's refusing to reveal details about the witnesses or evidence, so we have nothing new to go on."

"That's because there isn't any evidence. She's putting pressure on us, hoping we'll slip up and reveal a vital clue or get frustrated and make a confession."

"Cythera doesn't lie," Zandra said. "And when we spoke to Thelma, Emiline, and Clementine, they seemed convinced we'd done it, too."

"Emiline and Clementine were confused," I said. "They couldn't dredge up details of our fight with Agatha. Didn't you notice the glassy look in their eyes when we pressed for more information? That has to be magic-related. Someone cast a spell or a hex on them so they think they saw something they didn't."

"What if someone did that to us?" Zandra tugged on the ends of her hair. "Used magic to make us angry. What if I fought Agatha and Thelma, killed them, but I don't remember?"

"That's impossible. We're too powerful for such trickery to influence us. And no one could cast that kind of magic without lingering aftereffects, and I feel fine."

"I'm still suffering from drinking too many shots," Zandra said. "And not enough sleep. Or decent food. Everything feels wrong."

I hopped onto her lap and snuggled against her belly.

Unusually, she lifted me off.

"You don't want to be comforted?" I asked.

"Stop pretending there's not a problem between us," Zandra said. "You keep saying everything is weird, and whenever you do, I think about your magic."

I startled and stepped back. "My magic?"

"Yes. And there's no point in denying it. You've always hidden things from me. And that's been fine. We all have secrets or things in our past we're less than proud of, but it's gotten worse lately. When you gave me that enchanted bracelet so I'd forget, things changed between us. That was deceitful and wrong."

I gulped down my panic. "I didn't do it for a malicious reason. I needed more time."

"Time for what? To figure out how to keep deceiving me? Juno, we're bonded. We should share everything, but you've never let me in."

"I have! You're the most wonderful witch I've ever encountered. I couldn't imagine bonding with anyone else."

"You might have to," Zandra grumbled. "If these murder charges stick, we'll be separated. The angels won't risk keeping us together."

"That will never happen. I won't allow it." I rested a paw lightly on her leg. "I'm sorry if I've hurt your feelings."

She shuffled away. "You're always hiding things. I pretend not to care, but I do. It's not how it's supposed to be between us. Wiggles doesn't do that with Tempest."

"Wiggles? You can't compare us. He steals! He's excessively gassy. He became a father and hid it from Tempest."

"That's different. And he can't do anything about his gas."

"He could stop stealing gone-off food from the trash," I said. "And hiding his puppies was hardly a small thing."

"Wiggles did that because he was terrified of what Tempest would think about having a bundle of fire-breathing puppies romping around the apartment," Zandra said. "She's not exactly the motherly type."

An uneasy silence slid between us, coiling around my throat and making it tricky to swallow. Had my time just run out?

"I'm still unsure what you're implying about my magic." I did, but I wasn't willing to entertain the thought I'd broken something I couldn't fix.

Zandra was silent for a full minute. "What if the secrets you're hiding from me are behind the problems in Crimson Cove?"

I was stunned by her comment. "You think I'm a bad apple?"

Before Zandra could reply, the main door leading into the cells opened, and Cythera and Bertoli appeared.

I kept staring at Zandra, willing her not to be angry with me.

"It's no good ignoring me." Cythera stopped outside the cell door.

"I'm not. I'm busy with an urgent matter. You'll have to wait," I said.

Cythera hissed her anger. "We'll keep asking you the same thing until you confess."

"Give us ten minutes. We're in the middle of something."

"You don't get to make demands," Cythera snapped. "Will you behave, or do you need to be shackled?"

"We'll behave." Zandra slid off the bed and walked to the door.

I didn't want to go with the angels. I wanted to talk to Zandra about what she'd just said. My stomach was churning, and I felt light-headed. Zandra couldn't believe I was the problem behind this. We were a team. We always had each other's backs. Now, she doubted me.

I had to find a solution, but with Zandra refusing to so much as look at me, I followed her to the cell door, my head down.

Cythera and Bertoli led us into a quiet interview room, and we settled into chairs. We'd been questioned three times since they'd brought us in last night, and we'd repeated the same thing over and over. But they weren't happy with those answers.

"Now we've given you time to reconsider, let's try again," Cythera said. "Will you confess to the murders of Agatha and Thelma Black?"

"You can keep asking for as long as you like, and we'll keep denying it," I said.

"We need to test your magic," Cythera said.

"That will prove nothing," Zandra said. "You know we're powerful enough to commit these crimes."

"You used a dark spell," Cythera replied. "There could still be traces of it on your person.""That also won't help you," I said. "Dark magic has touched me more than once. The same for Zandra. It'll give you a false positive."

"Or it'll show us you're behind these troubles," Cythera said.

"Speaking of troubles, we've been discussing things," I said.Cythera arched an eyebrow. "Do you want to make a plea bargain?"

"No! Stop looking at these murders in isolation." I glanced at Zandra, but her expression was neutral, and she wouldn't look at me. "We believe someone is coming after the Crypt witches."

"That's hardly a surprise. They rub people the wrong way." There was a smirk on Cythera's face."Exactly! The Crypt witches are powerful and never back down from a fight. That has made them enemies," I said. "We believe someone is trying to bring them down and taking me along with them."

Cythera threw up her hands. "More lies! When will it end?"

"We had news there's trouble in Willow Tree Falls, much like Crimson Cove," I said. "Magic is misfiring, and the Crypt witches are struggling. The demon prison keeps failing, and their prisoners are getting out."

"We know," Cythera said. "I had a report from my colleague in Willow Tree Falls. Zandra's father has also been insistent on seeing her. He keeps saying he needs her free to help the family.""Why haven't we seen him?" I asked."You're to have no visitors until this matter is resolved.""You can't do that." Zandra stirred to life. "Dad will be worried about me.""He should be," Cythera said.

"You don't think it's odd that Willow Tree Falls and Crimson Cove are being targeted by malicious magic?" I asked. "There's a connection. Join the dots and they'll point you to the culprit."

"The connection is you two."

"Why would we want to bring down Zandra's family?" I shook with held in rage. "And Crimson

Cove is my home. We have friends here. We'd never hurt them."

"As you said, darkness has touched both of you. It corrupts. You've lost control. Committing these two murders is evidence of that," Cythera said.

"You know better than to make baseless accusations," I said. "Unless you tell us the facts, you'll get nothing out of us. We don't even know who found Thelma's body and when.""It wasn't long after you left her in that rental house," Bertoli said. "A passerby found her dead close to the front door. We believe she was attempting to escape and call for help or maybe tried to lock the doors to keep you out, but you found another way inside. Whatever she was trying to do, she failed."

"That's enough talking," Cythera said sharply. "We don't give criminals information that could help them. If you can't keep your mouth shut, go do some filing. Or do you want to find yourself on a suspension like your buddy, Finn?"

Bertoli mumbled an apology and looked at the floor.

There was a tense silence as neither side yielded. The silence could go on forever. I'd never yield to Angel Force intimidation tactics, because I was innocent.

"You may as well know some facts," Cythera said after much wing fluttering and sighing. "I'm going for banishment and magic stripping as your punishment. You deserve it. You escaped from my custody, and then a second murder happened. My reputation is in tatters because of your reckless acts."

I wrinkled my booping snooter. "Of course, we must think of your reputation first and foremost. We can't have the higher angels reprimanding you. You may get a demotion or lose your golden pension pot if you don't solve these murders quickly, so you're pinning it on the easiest suspects. That's bad policing. Shame on you."

Cythera smashed her fists against the table, causing the wood to groan. "Behave! Now isn't the time for games if you value your lives.""We're not playing," I growled out. "We know we didn't do this, but you need to allow us to clear our names. You never serve on the side of injustice."

"It's not happening. You're too much of a flight risk.""We can do nothing while we're stuck in a cell.""If I let you out, you could commit a dozen more murders," Cythera said."Where is the logic behind that ridiculous statement?" I asked. "We don't want to hurt anybody. We want to help them. That's what we do.""You want to cover your tracks and pretend you're innocent, the same as usual," Cythera said. "Not anymore. And I'm splitting you up. Perhaps, when you're alone, one of you will talk.""No! You can't do that," I said. "I won't be separated from Zandra."Zandra pushed back her chair. "It's a good idea. Maybe time apart will do us good. Are we done here?"

I blinked up at Zandra, shock curdling my insides. "You don't want to see me anymore?""I've got thinking to do, and so have you. Take me back to the cell."

My heart cracked as Zandra left me, escorted back to the cell by Bertoli. What would I do if my wonderful witch abandoned me for good?

Chapter 11

Alone

"You could always confess." Bertoli stood outside my cell. A cell I was in on my own. He'd been guarding me for hours, in between bouts of being asked the same questions by Cythera in her pointless attempt to discover I was a cold-hearted killer.

"If I did, nothing would change." I had my back to Bertoli, my heart hurting after Zandra's rejection, which made me want to curl into a fuzzy ball of despair and not move.

"It would make Cythera happy. I've never seen her like this," Bertoli said. "She's... scary."

"Everything in this town is scary. Haven't you been outside recently?"

"Are you sure you have nothing to do with this mess?" Bertoli asked after a second of hesitation.

I glanced over my shoulder at him. "We've had our differences, but even you know I'm not involved in these murders. I've made poor decisions, including some directed at you, but why would I kill strangers? It makes no sense."

Bertoli was quiet for a moment, just the gentle hum of the magic wards drifting around me. "Would you confess if it freed Zandra?"

I turned to face him and hissed. "That's a low blow. I'd do anything to protect my witch, but if I confess to these crimes, there'd still be a killer on the loose. You'd still have to deal with the problems Crimson Cove is facing and put other lives at risk."

He sighed. "There must be a reason all of this is happening."

"If you let me out, I'll help you find out what it is," I said. "Reunite me with Zandra, and we'll fix everything."

He shook his head. "She doesn't want to see you. I've told you that."

"And I don't believe you. Zandra would never abandon me. She's angry, and she has a right to be, but I'll make everything good. I need to see her, talk to her, convince her she's made a mistake."

"What if you're the one who's made a mistake?" Bertoli asked.

I flicked an ear. "I don't make mistakes."

"None of us are perfect. I know I'm not. I've done a lot of work on myself. It's made me see the world differently."

"Any errors I make, I learn from them," I said. "There's value in that."

"Then why isn't Zandra talking to you?" Bertoli asked. "It's got to be something big this time."

I wrinkled my booping snooter. "It's something I should have addressed a long time ago, but didn't know how."

"Your magic, you mean?"

I narrowed my eyes at him. "What do you know about my magic?"

Bertoli's piercing blue gaze skittered over me. "You're powerful. More powerful than most of us."

"And that's it?" I held my breath. Few people in Crimson Cove knew the full extent of my powers. Some of my magical misfits understood the basics, but the fewer people who knew, the safer it was for everybody.

"I know you're different from any other magic user I've met. It makes people wary around you, especially Cythera."

"She's wrong to think I'm the enemy," I said. "And if you believe I'm that powerful, then you should want me on your side."

"That almost sounds like a threat," Bertoli said.

"I'll start making threats if you prevent me from seeing Zandra—"

"It's not happening. Cythera wants to keep you apart, but Zandra wants a cell on her own. She wouldn't tell me why."

I sank low to the floor, refusing to give in to the despair that pressed heavily on my shoulders. I would make things right with my witch.

The main door leading into the cells opened, and a harried-looking angel poked his head through the gap. "Bertoli! We need you. Things are out of control in here."

"I'm guarding the prisoner," Bertoli said.

"Cythera said to get everybody. We need all hands on deck. They'll be fine."

"What's going on?" I asked.

The angel ignored me. "Hurry, before we lose control."

"Do nothing foolish," Bertoli warned me before jogging to the end of the corridor and through the door.

The second he was gone, I flung out a spell to bring down the magic wards. It pinged back and slammed into me, burning my fur. I growled and aimed more carefully, but the magic wards were strong and held against any spell I tried. Worse than that, my magic kept ricocheting off the wards and injuring me.

I paced beside the door, flicking my tail from side to side. There had to be a way out. I needed to get back to Zandra. And I didn't believe Bertoli. Zandra wanted to see me.

I turned to the back wall. I could blast through the bricks. There'd be magic wards on the exterior of the building, but it was unlikely Cythera had increased the wards everywhere. She was too distracted to think clearly. That was my way out. Once I was free, I'd grab Zandra, and we'd make a run for it.

I backed away until I almost touched the bars and summoned a lightning bolt between my paws. With careful aim, I thrust the lightning toward the wall at the back of my cell. It slammed into the bricks then turned back and aimed straight at me.

With an enraged yowl, I ducked and scrambled away, rolling under the small, fixed bed set against the wall to shield myself from the blast. As the lightning crackled into nothing, the floor vibrated.

"What now?" I murmured. Was a hellmouth opening and about to swallow the entire town? The way things were going, it wouldn't surprise me.

I scrambled out from under the bed just as the bricks on the external wall exploded inward. My spell had worked!

A few seconds later, a large furry head appeared through the gap. It was Archie!

"We thought you might need help," he said, his huge tongue lolling out of his mouth, a goofy grin on his face.

"Hurry, get inside before we're seen. The angels are coming."

That was Sammy!

More bricks exploded before Archie squeezed himself through the hole. He wagged his tail and attempted to lick the top of my head, which I avoided. Hellhound drool was pungent and sticky.

Sammy appeared next, looking disheveled and handsome. "We're here to break you out. But we can't go the way we came in. Angels spotted us when we breached the wall." He glowered at Archie. "Which we were supposed to do quietly."

"You can't quietly smash down a brick wall," Archie said. "I didn't growl or bark. That was me being quiet. I have no control over what the bricks did."

"We had magic that would have worked if you'd let me set it up," Sammy said. "We'll have to use it to open the cell door and go through the main building."

"While I appreciate the rescue, you'll get in trouble for helping me," I said.

"When we heard Angel Force had arrested you for two murders and were keeping you here, we knew something had gone wrong." Sammy gently bumped heads with me. "Angel Force is out of control. They're making arrests everywhere for no reason. They're targeting people at random and ignoring the criminals."

"They even went to Oak Park Ridge and tried to get the vampires, but Remus saw them off," Archie said.

"What have the vampires done wrong?" I asked.

"Nothing worse than usual. Cythera took a troop to get in, but she failed. I may have been involved in chasing them away. Angels taste so sweet. Like chewing on salted caramel toffee."

"You might want to duck for this bit." Sammy backed away from the cell bars, crouching low on his belly.

There was a loud pop, a fizzing sound, and an enormous sparkle of stars. The cell door swung open.

"Let's move," Sammy said.

"Wait! I need to find Zandra," I said.

"They're still in here." An angel poked his head through the hole in the wall and shot out a spell.

"No time." Sammy shoved me out the open door, Archie taking the lead.

"I need to get to Zandra," I insisted. "The angels separated us, and they're saying she doesn't want to talk to me."

"We'll get her, but we need to get ourselves out first," Sammy said. "Get a move on. Those angels are right on my tail, and I don't want it blasted off!"

More spells skimmed over our heads, so we had no choice but to hustle. Archie slammed through the door at the end of the corridor, skidding to a halt as we emerged into the open-plan office.

It was bedlam. There were several fights, some going on between angels. Smoke billowed out of the kitchen. Someone shattered a large glass window, causing everyone to jump, and a pile of files caught fire and vanished into ash.

"Prisoner on the loose!" the angel behind us yelled.

Archie's massive form blocked his way, his fiery red eyes glowing with fury, tail lashing. Sammy, usually the calmest of us, had his magic ready, a faint blue light flickering from his paws.

I nudged them into action before we got cornered by a bunch of angry angels, and we were soon leaping over desks, avoiding attempts at being grabbed, and heading to the exit.

Three angels fired up their magic and blocked our escape.

"Let's try the back way." I skidded around, and we dashed back through the chaos, dodging another fire and three angels pummeling each other for an unknown reason. We'd just made it to the corridor that would take us past the small morgue and to the back door when we were forced to stop.

There were angels in front and behind us. We'd been cut off.

My heart raced as I eyed the angels, but I kept my breath steady. No time to panic now.

One angel stepped forward, wings flaring.

I glanced at Sammy, who was flexing a paw, getting ready to cast something.

"Archie, Sammy, get ready," I warned. "They want me. I'll hold them off while you run."

Before we could react, the angel lunged, a blur of white and feathers. I barely dodged in time, throwing myself out of his way. Sammy flicked his tail, and the air pulsed with raw energy as a shield formed around us.

Archie wasn't waiting for orders. With a snarl, he charged at the nearest angel, his massive form barreling toward the enemy. He leaped, jaws snapping, but the angel sidestepped with unnerving grace, wings flapping with a force that sent Archie tumbling to the floor.

The other angels were closing in, their eyes glowing with righteous fury.

I didn't have time to think. I had to act.

With a quick flick of my whiskers, I summoned my magic, hoping it would hold and not let me down when I most needed it. For once, it curled around me like an old friend hugging me. I thrust my paws forward, and the air crackled as a bolt of light shot out, striking the lead angel in the chest. He staggered back but absorbed the blow and barely flinched.

Sammy sent a burst of magical fire toward one angel, the flames licking at her wings. But the angel swatted it away with a single sweep of her arm, her blue eyes narrowing.

We couldn't take them all down, not like this. The angels were too strong, and there were too many of them. Confined in this corridor, we had limited options of where to go.

"We need a distraction," I muttered to Sammy.

He nodded, already gathering energy for his next move.

I didn't wait for him to finish. I threw myself at the nearest angel, claws extended, using my agility to slip past his defenses. I darted between his legs, staying low, and swiped my claws across his leg. It made the angel stagger, his attention briefly distracted.

"Now, Sammy!" I shouted.

Sammy released a massive burst of magical energy, creating an explosion of light and sound that filled the corridor. The angels reeled back, disoriented. The blast sent one of them crashing into the wall.

"Archie, run through them!" I yelled.

Archie was on his paws, charging with all his might. He barreled into the nearest angel, knocking her out of the air with a bone-rattling thud.

That show of force made the others hesitate, and that was all we needed.

With a final surge of magic, I smashed a hole through the door at the end of the corridor.

"Go!" I commanded.

Archie shoved the nearest angel away, Sammy right behind him, and we all leaped through the hole. I felt a tug of magic pulling me back. The wards must have sensed I was a prisoner about to flee, but I fought it with howls and my vicious murder mittens, slashing, snarling, and hissing.

The magic broke with a fizzle, and I rolled to my paws.

We didn't stop to see if we were being followed but raced away, out of sight of the angels. We ducked into an alley close to Vorana's bookstore to take a moment to gather ourselves and figure out our next move.

"I should go back for Zandra," I said. "I don't want her to think I'm abandoning her."

"She'll be fine where she is," Sammy said. "You're my priority. We need to get you somewhere safe. You'll be no use to Zandra if you're behind bars. You find the evidence to clear your names, and then you can get Zandra out."

"Where should we go?" I asked. "Angel Force will look for me everywhere."

"To my house." Archie checked no one was watching before slipping out of the alley and motioning with his head for us to follow. "The vampires won't let anything bad happen to us. Although I should warn you, they're extra spicy. Make sure you don't get too close."

"The vampires are out of control too?" I asked, double-checking it was safe to move.

"Everyone is," Sammy said. "Even I feel weird. I get waves of anger rolling over me, and then they fade. And Archie tried to bite me several times."

Archie whimpered. "I didn't mean to, but this rage hits, and I can't control myself. I always say sorry when I try to rip your head off."

"None of us are in our right minds. Which is why we have to fix Crimson Cove," Sammy said.

"I'm glad you could control yourselves enough to get me out," I said. "The angels are certain we murdered those witches."

"Which you didn't, right?" Archie asked.

"Of course they didn't," Sammy said. "Did you? No offense, but with everyone's magic off-kilter, we're all doing things we're not proud of."

"It wasn't us," I said. "We were unlucky and had a run-in with those witches as soon as they arrived in Crimson Cove. Actually, it was more of a run-over since my tail got squashed by their broken limousine. But we sorted everything. We even had a fun evening together the night Agatha was killed."

"Everyone is saying otherwise," Sammy said, keeping up a brisk pace as we left behind the town and headed to the Crimson Cove border on the road that would take us into Oak Park Ridge.

"What is the gossip grapevine saying?" I asked.

"That you fought with the witches and then stalked them that same night to get revenge."

"That didn't happen," I said. "I've tried telling Cythera everything, but she's not interested in the truth. She has us pegged as guilty, and that's all she cares about."

"Let's get somewhere quiet and figure things out," Sammy said.

We dashed the rest of the way to Oak Park Ridge in silence. My senses were on high alert, the atmosphere pricking at me. It was almost as bad when we got to Oak Park Ridge. There were waves of strange energy surrounding us.

"We should stay outside," Archie said before barreling into a specially made passageway through the thick brick wall into the grounds of Remus's estate. "It's getting late, so the vampires will be active. I don't want to fight any of them. Not like last night."

"You've been fighting your family to stay safe?" I asked.

"They don't mean it. They seem extra hungry," Archie said. "I've blasted a few with fireballs as a warning, and that keeps them away. If anyone comes for you, use fire. Otherwise, run as fast as you can."

I looked around for signs of stalking vampires. Maybe coming here wasn't such a good idea.

"There's an old folly I use," Archie said. "We'll go there. The vampires don't like it, because it's not fancy enough for them."

We hurried on. I kept glancing around, looking for signs of danger. There were no vampires, but I got that creeping sensation down my spine, suggesting we were being watched. I slowed and carefully scanned our surroundings. I couldn't see anyone, but I was convinced we were being observed.

"Do you sense vampires close by?" I asked.

Archie lifted his enormous head and inhaled deeply. "There's no one out here. They take ages to preen, so we're good for now. Remus takes a whole hour to decide which suit to wear."

"I feel like we're being observed. Do you not sense it?" I asked.

"I've been so jumpy recently. I don't know if it's me being paranoid or some creeper lurking close by," Sammy said. "I haven't been able to relax for weeks."

We continued walking and reached Archie's folly a few moments later. It stood at the far end of an overgrown patch of garden, its stone façade weathered and worn. Ivy crawled up the sides, intertwining with the cracked stone.

As I entered, a faint scent of moss and damp earth clung to the air. Nature had almost reclaimed this place. The interior was a chaotic mess of saggy furniture and blankets, all well-used by Archie and covered in his fur.

"Pick a cushion. Or a blanket. Don't use the red chair. That's where the mice live," he said.

While they settled in, I remained by the door, looking outside. Someone was watching us! I saw a flash of movement, but it was gone as quickly as it appeared.

"What does Angel Force have on you?" Sammy asked as he sniffed at the cushion he perched on, his nose wrinkled. "Anyone I've spoken to is convinced you and Zandra were involved in these murders."

"Cythera keeps saying there are witnesses." I was still looking out the door. "She won't give names or any details, but she said people saw Zandra fighting with Agatha Black on the night she died. But she was alive when we left the bar."

"I heard she was missing when you left the bar," Sammy said.

I gave him a sharp look. "Do you doubt my word?"

"No! But people are saying you killed Agatha and then left the bar, making a show of leaving, so it would seem as if you'd been there the whole time."

"There's no motive, though," I said.

"You getting run over by their hired car is a decent motive."

I hissed at Sammy. "Agatha's friend Emiline healed my tail. All was forgiven."

"What about the other witch? Thelma?" Archie asked. "Someone told me you visited her, and then she died. There's even a rumor you scared her to death."

"We went to see Thelma to find out what she knew about the fight that was supposed to have happened," I said. "When we arrived, she was scared and seemed convinced we were involved, but she had no details. It was the same when we spoke to Emiline and Clementine, their friends. Neither had information on what happened, just a vague idea we fought Agatha. And we only learned what happened to Thelma when Cythera tracked us down while we were interviewing possible suspects."

"What other suspects have you got?" Sammy asked.

"No one concrete. We spoke to Thelma, Clementine, and Emiline. Agatha and Thelma's boyfriends and Mrs. Wick. She was their employer. We couldn't find a solid motive for any of them."

"When I first heard a dark-haired witch you knew had died, I was worried. Of course, I shouldn't have been." Archie yanked a jumbo bone from under a cushion and gnawed the end.

"Why would that be?" I asked.

"For a second, I thought Zandra was the dead witch. Someone described the victim as pale with dark hair and seen hanging around with you."

I tilted my head. "I suppose, from the back, they looked similar. Dark hair. Jeans. The sisters had a similar style to Zandra, although they liked more sparkle. Zandra isn't a sparkly witch."

"I tried to find you to make sure everything was okay. That's when I heard the angels were interested in you for the murder," Archie said. "I knew then Zandra was alive. You'd never hurt your bonded witch."

I twitched my whiskers. "Of course not. I'd protect her with my life."

Archie nodded. "We protect those we bond with. Even when they try to bite us."

"Did you get any useful information out of Angel Force?" Sammy asked.

"Finn let us look at Agatha's body. There were no marks on her, so we know magic ended her life. I need access to the tests done on both the bodies to see if I can narrow down the type of spell used."

"How will you do that? If we risk going back to Angel Force, we'll all be arrested," Sammy said.

"I'll get the information. I never give up when I want something." And since these murders put freedom at risk for me and Zandra, I wouldn't stop until I succeeded.

Chapter 12

Finding allies

"I hate this." Archie whimpered and crouched beside me. "They'll see us. I'm too large to hide under this spell. It doesn't feel safe. It keeps wobbling, and my tail pokes out. I have a unique tail. Anyone who sees my tail will know I'm hiding."

"The magic is holding, at least for now," I whispered. "We must do this. We need access to the information Angel Force has on Agatha and Thelma. What if you're right and there is a connection to Zandra?"

Since Archie had mentioned how similar Agatha and Thelma looked to Zandra when you saw them from behind, I couldn't stop thinking about it. I wanted it to be wrong. Someone wasn't coming after Zandra, were they? But link that possibility to the disruption in Willow Tree Falls, and I was concerned. I had to be certain Zandra wasn't vulnerable. Until I was sure, I wouldn't rest.

"Incoming," Sammy whispered. He was crouched beside me, his eyes wide as we waited in the alley opposite Angel Force under a concealment spell.

"More angels," I hissed softly. "Not regulars."

A group of unfamiliar angels landed on the street. There were twenty of them, including several warrior angels with steel-tipped wings carrying battle swords.

"Cythera means business if she's bringing in warriors," Sammy said. "We won't get inside if they're guarding the place."

"I'm not giving up on Zandra," I said. "I need all the information on what happened to Agatha and Thelma. We'll get it."

We were quiet as the newly arrived angels trooped inside the building to get their orders. Top of their list would be to find and apprehend me.

"We could try an invisibility spell," Sammy said.

"What if it fails when we're inside?" Archie asked. "Magic keeps doing the opposite of what it's supposed to. It could hold out until we're at our most vulnerable, and then—poof—we're revealed in front of all those mean-looking angels."

"Then we fight our way out again," I said.

"Or end up behind bars for the rest of our lives, forced to eat tasteless gruel forever." Archie hid his muzzle under a giant paw.

"Remus would break you out."

"He might, but he's been distracted and hungry. I've been afraid to be around him," Archie said.

"He's that bad?" I glanced at my always loyal friend.

"All the vampires are tetchy." Archie huffed out a smoky breath. "You didn't hear this from me, but there's been illegal feeding going on. I've had to help hide the bodies."

"Whatever is messing with Crimson Cove is stretching as far as Oak Park Ridge," I said. "This is powerful magic we're dealing with."

"It must be if it's affecting you and the vampires," Sammy said. "You told us your spells have been going wrong."

"That's nothing new. My magic has been malfunctioning for a long time."

Sammy looked at me with a curious expression on his face but didn't press for more information.

"We could try round the back," Archie said. "Maybe they haven't shored up the hole we made. We could pop through and get into the office, nab the information, escape, and then stop for snacks."

"We need the information on the bodies, but we also need Zandra," I said. "The angels will know I'll return for her, so they'll be on high alert. That could be why they've recruited the warrior angels."

There was a flurry of activity inside Angel Force. Bertoli appeared with several of the new angels, issuing instructions and pointing out directions. The three angels he was with took to the wing and vanished, leaving Bertoli standing alone.

"He'll do," I said. "We'll get the information from Bertoli."

"I didn't think he liked you," Sammy said.

"We have an uneasy truce. It's as good as it's going to get. I can't rely on Finn for the information since

Cythera suspended him. Let's follow Bertoli. We'll get him in a quiet place and convince him to help."

We slunk along together, keeping a tight formation to ensure we remained under the spell. The magic trembled, threatening to break and reveal us, but it held as we walked away from Angel Force.

Bertoli kept up a brisk pace, looking like he was heading home. He slowed twice and looked over his shoulder as if sensing we were following him. Every time he did, we froze, and I checked the magic still held. It was unnatural to doubt such a simple spell, but I had to doubt everything to keep everyone safe.

Despite the late hour, the streets hummed with activity. There were lights on in most of the houses we walked by and clear signs chaos ruled, with smashed windows and damaged vehicles abandoned on the street. I even spotted the limousine that had crushed my tail. Smoke billowed from beneath the hood.

"Bertoli's going home," I whispered. "We'll wait until he unlocks his front door and bundle him inside. Then we can talk with no one seeing."

Bertoli had an apartment in a small, tidy complex, close to his work. He unlocked the access to the main door, and once he was inside, Archie jammed a paw in to make sure it didn't shut so we could get through.

We crept behind Bertoli as he headed to his front door and inserted the key. The second he opened the door, we charged.

Bertoli yelped as Archie knocked him off his feet, and he landed face down in his hallway.

"Hurry, close the door. We don't want anyone to hear," I said.

Sammy nudged Bertoli's feet out of the way and eased the front door shut.

"What's going on? Who's there? I can hear you!" Bertoli was rolling around on the floor, pinned under one of Archie's giant paws.

I dropped the cover spell.

Bertoli gaped at me. "Juno! You're in so much trouble."

"I'm not here to harm you," I said. "I need your help. We have a new theory, and it's one I'm unhappy about, but I must pursue it."

"I can't help you. I'd lose my job!" Bertoli blasted out magic, knocking Archie off his paws, and I barely had time to register Bertoli's sword before it was swinging at me.

Archie let out a bone-rattling growl, his form filling the hallway with heat as he lunged, massive jaws snapping at Bertoli.

Bertoli swiped a hand through the air, sending Archie tumbling back, his fur singed by a burst of angel fire.

I leaped at Bertoli's throat to distract him from attacking Archie. I needed this angel alive so I wouldn't inflict serious damage, but he needed to know we weren't messing around.

He spun, wings flaring, and my magic crashed into his wing shield, sending a shockwave through the apartment. Glass shattered. A lamp exploded.

Sammy hissed out a bolt of blue lightning, hitting Bertoli and making him drop his sword.

Archie was back on his paws, charging at Bertoli again. I dove in, murder mittens slashing. The hallway lit up in a fiery flash, and Bertoli yelped as Archie clamped down on his arm.

"Enough! Stop!" Bertoli held a hand up in a show of submission.

"You started this fight. We only wanted to talk," I said. "And since when have you had a sword?"

"I got advanced training recently." Bertoli winced as Archie drooled on his arm, his teeth still embedded. "I had academy training, but I was rusty. Cythera is making us carry swords to protect ourselves."

"Not from us," I said.

"You followed me home and jumped me! I knew I was being watched."

"Because we couldn't risk you sounding the alarm before we talked." I could see the hesitation in the angel's eyes. "Bertoli, I need your help. I'm innocent of murder, and I have nowhere else to turn."

"And you want me to fix your mess?" Bertoli glared at Archie. "Get off me. I can't talk when I'm worried I'm about to lose a limb."

"That last spell hurt," Archie said. "My leg is still tingling."

I gestured for Archie to let go, and Bertoli scrambled away and hauled himself into a chair in the living room. He ran his hands through his hair several times and took a moment to inspect his wings and arm.

Archie followed Bertoli then stopped and lifted his nose. "Do I smell cookies?"

"I bake," Bertoli said. "It's a stress reliever. I've been baking a lot recently."

Archie wagged his tail. "Can I have some cookies?"

"No! You don't deserve a treat after you tried to chew off my arm."

"Please," Archie whined. "I'm starving. Chasing angels always makes me hungry."

"Anything makes you hungry," Sammy muttered.

Bertoli sighed. "In the kitchen on the counter, in the tin with the rabbits. Don't eat them all! In fact, bring them here. I need sugar after what you've just put me through."

"Are there snacks for us?" I asked.

"You are unbelievable," Bertoli said.

"I've been evading capture. That leaves little time for snacks and meals."

Bertoli shook his head. "Archie, if you can figure out how to open the fridge, bring in the packet of salmon. It's pre-cooked. It was supposed to be my dinner."

"You're literally an angel," I said.

We took a moment to replenish with snacks while I kept a watchful eye on Bertoli. A flicker of hope lit inside me. Would he be our ally? Or was this a trick to deceive us, allowing him time to figure out how to contact Angel Force and recapture me?

"The cookies are amazing." Archie danced on his paws, cookie crumbs on the floor. "You're an incredible baker."

"Thanks." Bertoli brushed crumbs off his fingers and focused on me. "I know something weird is going on in Crimson Cove. Cythera and Finn are behaving strangely. I want to hear your theory behind it."

"Cythera often behaves strangely," I said. "But you're right. She's different. Sharper. Scarier."

"And Finn," Bertoli said, "I kept telling Cythera his demon side is getting stronger, but she doesn't care. She's always been on Finn's tail to make sure he controls his darker side. She was even reluctant to hire him because of his parents."

"That is an unwelcome shift in her behavior," I said.

Bertoli tipped back his head. "Our town is in chaos. Every time we solve one crime, two more pop up. It doesn't matter how many angels we throw at it. We won't resolve this situation while we're stamping out the symptoms instead of finding the cause of all this chaos."

"I agree," I said. "That's what I've been trying to do. That's what I want to do."

"I... I think I believe you. I want to," Bertoli said.

"When have I ever done anything to make you doubt me?"

His smile was wry. "I often doubt you. But I know you'd do nothing to put Zandra in harm's way."

"On that, we agree."

"You mentioned a new theory?" Bertoli asked.

I settled on a soft blue blanket. "Archie drew my attention to how similar Agatha and Thelma look to Zandra."

Bertoli's eyebrows lifted. "I noticed the same thing. They could all be sisters."

"That idea has me panicked," I said. "What if the killer thought they were attacking Zandra when they went after Agatha and then Thelma?"

"You think the killer targeted the wrong witches?" Bertoli exhaled sharply. "It's possible. And how they were hit with magic makes it even more so."

"What have you learned?" I leaned forward.

"We've done more tests on Agatha and Thelma. The lingering magic is strongest on their backs and in their hair."

"Which means they were attacked from behind!" I drew in a shaky breath. "The killer could easily have mistaken Agatha and Thelma for Zandra. When we met, they wore almost identical outfits, minus the sparkles and feather boas, and they have the same long, dark hair and pale skin."

"They could have made that mistake," Bertoli said.

My heart plummeted to my paws and bounced back up into my throat. "I need to get Zandra out of Angel Force. I must protect her. If the killer is targeting her, they'll try again."

Bertoli shook his head. "Zandra is in the safest place."

"Your cells aren't that safe," I said. "I got busted out easily enough."

"We fixed that error," Bertoli said, shooting a glare at Archie and Sammy. "We have warrior angels on-site, and more are coming. Zandra should stay where she is. She's in a heavily guarded cell, surrounded by protective magic wards. If you break her out, you'll be on your own. You'll have no protection from Angel Force. In fact, you'll have us tracking you, along with whoever wants her dead."

"But who wants to murder Zandra?" Sammy asked.

"We've been working on a theory that someone is targeting the Crypt witches," I said. "Zandra's sister, Tempest, was framed for murder. And when I was around her, I noticed a distortion in her magic. It faded, but she's not stable. And there's trouble in Willow Tree Falls, where the Crypt witches have their demon prison. Their magic is failing, and the demons are breaking out. This isn't an isolated incident. The Crypt witches are in trouble."

"I promise I can better protect Zandra while she's in our custody. I'll monitor the cell wards and make sure she has limited contact with any other angel," Bertoli said.

I was torn. Part of me wanted Zandra by my side, but she had a safe layer of protection tucked away inside Angel Force.

Bertoli sat forward. "Trust me, just like I am you. I won't let you down. You need to focus on finding out what's wrong with Crimson Cove before it's too late for all of us. Angel Force is teetering on the brink of anarchy, and the rest of the town is following. We've almost lost control."

"If someone is coming after the Crypt witches and can influence their magic, it means they're immensely powerful," Sammy said.

"Even with the extra angels, we may not be able to bring them down." Bertoli fixed me with a stern look. "Juno, I know you hold back. You have more power than I've ever experienced, and that's not even you operating at full force. If anyone can stop this, it's you. This town is relying on you. We can't rely on Angel Force anymore. Cythera is doing her best, but she's struggling, and the angels are suffering. This whole town is suffering."

"My magic isn't what it once was," I said. "I'm not as strong as I used to be. And the pernicious slime squelching through our beloved town is messing with me, too."

"You can do this," Sammy said. "And we'll help."

"Of course we will," Archie said. "We always help our friends. Especially when they reward us with snacks!"

I made a decision. "For now, Zandra stays where she is. However, I need access to the case files on Agatha and Thelma. I must know everything if I'm to catch who did this."

Bertoli pressed his lips together. "I can get them. You wait here. It'll be easy for me to sneak in during the chaos and grab the files while no one is watching."

"Are there any more cookies while we wait?" Archie asked.

Bertoli scowled at him. "You must have a bottomless pit for a stomach. I saw you steal the last cookie."

"And he nabbed some of my salmon," Sammy grumbled.

Archie whimpered and lowered his head.

"Fine! There are cheese scones and a strawberry upside-down cake in the kitchen. Save me a slice."

Archie danced with glee and dashed to the kitchen.

I walked Bertoli to the front door and placed a firm paw on his booted foot. "I'm trusting you. Don't let me down."

"Likewise. Everyone thinks you're guilty, and I'm still uncertain about you."

"You're my last hope, Bertoli. I would never deceive you when it involves keeping Zandra safe."

Bertoli slid out of the door. By the time I'd returned to the living room, Archie was devouring the entire strawberry upside-down cake while Sammy nibbled a cheese scone.

"Do you trust him?" Sammy asked as he pushed a fresh scone my way.

"I'm all out of trust right now. We'll watch out the window. If any angels descend from the skies, we'll run."

It was a tense twenty minutes before I saw Bertoli dashing back to the apartment. He was alone, and I let out a relieved sigh.

Ten minutes later, we all sat on the floor, looking through Thelma and Agatha's case files.

"These are the notes on the magic used to kill them." Bertoli set several pages in front of me.

I read through the information, and my eyes widened. "This is a rare and powerful combination of magic."

"It was probably stronger, but there's a fade to it. By the time we took samples, I estimate fifty percent of whatever magic was used to murder them had gone," Bertoli said.

"We're talking about an uber-powerful magic user," Archie said. He was sitting on the empty plate that once held the cake, too ashamed to admit he'd eaten it all.

"Something ancient and powerful," I murmured.

"Have you ever seen this magic before?" Bertoli focused intently on me.

"A long time ago, but this kind of power is outlawed, and there's no one alive who can use it. At least, there shouldn't be."

"I figured you'd know something about it," Bertoli said.

I glanced at him. "Why do you say that?"

"Because you use spells and magic I've never seen before, and I've been around for a while. If the magic that killed Agatha and Thelma is old and powerful, you most likely know about it."

"That's because Juno's smart." Archie let out an indelicate strawberry-scented burp. "She's something else."

Bertoli stood. "You'll see from the autopsy notes that the magic was most concentrated on the victims' backs."

I closed my eyes for a second. The killer *was* after my wonderful witch. This investigation had just gotten intensely personal.

"I've got to go back to work," Bertoli said. "Cythera caught me in the office. She wants me to go to the hospital. Do you remember Charlie, Randal's friend, who got caught up in the attack at his house?"

"Of course," I said.

"Well, he's woken up."

"That's good news."

"I hope so. I need to see if he remembers anything about that night. Stay here for as long as you need," Bertoli said. "But be careful when you leave. No one can connect us, or I'll find myself behind bars and have my wings taken."

"We'll be discreet." Archie wagged his tail and knocked over a lamp.

Bertoli sighed. "And control your kittens, Juno. I keep seeing them around town misbehaving. There have been complaints."

I nodded, but my focus was on the autopsy files and test results. I had bigger things to worry about than three tiny fire-breathing fluff babies.

Chapter 13

Truth time

A weak sun lifted over Crimson Cove as I snuck into Vorana's bookstore with Sammy and Archie. Vorana had books about everything, from obscure magical chants to the latest thriller crammed with powerful witches and their amazing sidekicks. I often wondered why no one had asked me to be in such an epic series.

I hoped there'd be something between the pages to help us figure out what magic was used to kill Agatha and Thelma. Figure out the spell, narrow down the candidates who could cast it.

"If we're talking old magic," Sammy said as he browsed along the bookshelves, "this is the section we need."

We focused on that stack and spent a few minutes browsing the shelves, pulling down useful books with our paws and noses.

Archie huffed as he nudged a massive tome off a low shelf, sending up a puff of dust that made Sammy sneeze.

I pressed my paw against the cover to flip it open and used my booping snooter to nudge the delicate pages, scanning for anything useful.

Sammy batted at the edges of a book with his paw, sending pages flopping wildly before Archie grumbled and held the spine steady with an enormous paw.

"This would be easier if we had thumbs," Sammy muttered as he squinted at the text.

Archie let out a deep-chested woof of agreement then used his snout to push another book toward me. The words were in a looping script, some glowing faintly with old magic. I leaned in close as I read.

The store was silent except for the occasional rustle of pages and the faint creaks of the wooden shelves settling around us.

"This book is about curses. Some of them are horrible." Archie lay flat on his belly, his nose brushing along the pages as he slowly read, taking his time over each word.

"It must have been an illegal spell," I said. "It could have been a curse that killed Agatha and Thelma."

There was a soft thump, and something or someone landed on the floor. I tensed, and my head whipped over to the front door, but it was closed.

"Did you hear that?" I whispered to the others.

"I can only focus on one thing at a time," Archie said. "Some of these words are long. What's a prognosticating augur?"

"A future vision," Sammy whispered, his gaze tracking me. "Juno, what do you sense?"

I crept to the end of the bookstack and peered around the corner just as a wave of magic swept over me, sending tingles from my booping snooter to the tip of my tail.

Light flared, and I spotted Sage rearing up in her harness, magic blazing between her paws.

"Stop! It's us!" I ran toward her so she could see we were no threat and wouldn't unleash a no doubt epic spell to protect the bookstore.

Sage's furious expression shifted to confusion, and she slumped to the floor. "Are you trying to get yourself killed? What are you doing breaking into Vorana's bookstore?"

I stood over her as she shook and panted. "What's wrong with you?"

"Nothing. I've not been sleeping well. And it doesn't help when I get an alert that there's trouble in the store. You know Vorana has this place warded."

"It's more than that," I said. "You're freezing, and your gums are pale."

Sage pulled back as I inspected her almost-white gums. "I'm lacking sleep because of those treacherous kittens. You promised to find them a home, yet they're still being mini menaces! I shut my eyes, and they're on me."

"And I will. In case you don't know what's going on, I'm busy trying to save this town and Zandra," I said.

"I know what's happening." Sage shivered so hard her harness rattled. "You still haven't told me what you're doing here."

"Old friend, we mean no harm." I sat beside her. "I got access to the case files on the two murdered witches, and we're pinning down what type of magic was used to kill them. I knew Vorana's resources would help."

Sage grunted and grumbled, unable to settle into a comfortable cat-loaf position. "I'd offer to assist, but I'm worse than useless. That last spell almost knocked me out. I have no energy. It's a sign of old age."

"Nonsense. You're being affected by what's blighting this town." I gently patted Sage on the head. "Go snuggle under a blanket and keep warm. Do you want something to eat?"

"I have no appetite. I keep worrying about Vorana and how I can't protect her."

"She's safe where she is," I said.

"That house doesn't feel safe," Sage said. "Not after you brought a pack of angry wild dogs to the door."

"They haven't been back, have they?"

"No, but that's not the point. Trouble follows you around. And have you seen Zandra's mother recently?"

"Adrienne hasn't been by in a couple of weeks. I assumed she was off having an adventure with Joel."

"She's around. And she's being snappy. A snappy ghoul is a dangerous ghoul. It's a bad look on her. I chased her away when she tried to get into the house and then strengthened the wards. I don't know how long I can keep them up, though. Once the wards fall, we're goners. If it's not the crazed wild dogs, it'll be the hungry ghouls."

"I'm sorry Adrienne has been bothering you. She must be looking for Zandra. Perhaps she senses she's in trouble." I sighed. "We can't seem to catch a break on this case, and Angel Force is closing in."

"I've been listening to the gossip. I don't believe you and Zandra had anything to do with those witches' deaths." Sage yawned, pulled a blanket off one of the easy chairs, and burrowed under it. "I'm about the only one who believes that, though. Your name is being dragged through the mud. Zandra's too."

"We must find the source of the magic," I said. "When I looked at Agatha's body, I could tell ancient, powerful magic had been used to kill her. No one should be casting magic like that."

"If it's any help, I'm in charge of the bookstore, so you can take all the time you need to check the books. I can keep the place closed. After the recent brawls and all the shoplifting, it's safest that way," Sage said.

"Is Vorana not coming in?" I asked.

"Vorana's in bed. She's tired and sick. So am I. I'm only doing this because I'm devoted to my witch."

"Huh. Who's caring for the kittens?"

Sage thumped me with a paw. "You're supposed to be! They're under your care, yet I've barely seen you at the house, let alone looking after those monsters."

I had the decency to duck my head. "They can't be causing that much trouble."

"They are. You need to come home and sort your mess," Sage said.

"It'll be risky returning to Vorana's. Angel Force could be watching the house, expecting me to go back."

"Then take the risk. I need your help!" Sage said. "And I'm worried about Vorana. I don't have the energy to protect her anymore. I'm fading. So is she."

I'd never abandon a friend in need, and Vorana had been good to Zandra and me since we'd moved to Crimson Cove.

"Archie, stay here and keep reading. Put aside anything you find useful. I'll take Sammy and Sage back to Vorana's and see how she's doing."

"And you'll dig out those pesky kittens and box them sharply around the ears. I'm not a target for their fireballs," Sage said.

"I'll set them straight, but I didn't think they were home," I said. "Bertoli told me they'd been seen causing mischief in town."

"They come and go. And that's the problem. I can't relax because I never know when they'll reappear and jump on me. They're always attacking. Each time they do, they feel stronger, while I get weaker."

"Let's go see what we can do. We won't be long, Archie," I said.

He nodded, his focus intent on a book. "I'll let you know if I find anything good. Be safe."

"Do you have enough energy to magic us to Vorana's house?" I asked Sage.

"Not a chance. We're walking," Sage said. "If I try a translocation spell, who knows where we could end up? Or even if we'd reappear."

"Then we do this the old-fashioned way. Paw power."

We snuck out of the bookstore and hurried along the street. It was quiet since it was early, but there were stirrings of life, and I kept a sharp lookout for angel flybys. They might spot us and swoop down, thwarting my plans. Although I was still uncertain which direction those plans were headed.

We made it back to Vorana's house unnoticed. It took Sage several seconds to unlock the magic wards around the house before we could get inside.

"That's a lot of magic wrapped around this place," Sammy said.

"It's extra protection," Sage said. "I've even suggested to Vorana we leave until things return to normal, but she won't hear it. Although, I think she was delirious when she said that. I'm worried about her."

"Her sickness could be connected to yours," I said. "Your bond is one of the strongest I've ever seen. If she's not feeling well, it makes sense you won't either."

"I'll stand guard down here," Sammy said, "keep an eye on everything and watch out for any angels."

I gave him an affectionate head nudge and then hurried up the stairs, with Sage floating behind me, her harness occasionally clanking against the wooden steps.

The second we entered Vorana's bedroom, I could tell she was sick. There was a faint musky smell, and a fog swirled around Vorana's bed.

"How long has she been like this?" I asked Sage.

"It comes and goes," Sage said. "I don't know what the fog is. I can't get rid of it. No spells touch it. I even opened the window, but it won't drift out."

I hopped onto Vorana's bed. She lay shivering under the covers, although when I touched her skin, it was hot. "Vorana, it's Juno. Can you hear me?"

She moaned softly. "Need to get up—"

"You're staying here," I said. "You're very unwell. I didn't realize things had gotten this bad."

"It came on suddenly," Sage said, floating up to join me on the bed. "One minute, she was complaining about the toaster going wrong again, and then she fainted. It took me ages to bring her round. I got her up here after much struggling and protesting, and we've been here ever since."

"Go. Got to leave," Vorana whispered.

"Not until you're well," I said. "Stay here, where we can protect you. What's this on her arms?" Small, red, inflamed-looking pinpricks marked Vorana's arms.

"They appeared overnight," Sage said. "I wondered if they were vampire bites, but they're too small."

"I know Remus's vampires are misbehaving, but you're right. A vampire wouldn't make these marks." I sniffed the marks and recoiled.

Sage shivered as she snuggled close to Vorana. "I can't heal her. My magic isn't working. It's as if our connection is warped."

"You still feel your bond, though?" I asked.

"It's there, but it's shaky. It wants to break. If I can't heal Vorana, then I'll stay and die with her."

"It won't come to that. Never give up on your bonded magic user," I said. "I suspect Vorana's illness is linked to whatever's going on in town. Yours too."

"Will everyone go the same way?" Sage asked after a few seconds of hesitation. "We'll all get sick and fail?"

"I can't say for certain, but everyone is acting out of character," I said. "Cythera is being intensely irrational and unkind. I've never seen her like this. And the vampires are breaking the rules and feeding when they shouldn't. Even Finn is struggling with his demon side. And then there was the fight in Vorana's store. The bookstore is a place of peace. No one would ever fight over a book."

"Vorana would." Sage grimaced. "But not at the moment. The town is being flipped on its head. There must be a solution. But if it's as complicated as whatever magic has Vorana in a chokehold, I don't know how anyone can fix this."

"I will. I'm determined to free Zandra, clear our names, and fix the town. I'll make sure Crimson Cove is back to how it should be. Vorana included."

Sage didn't look convinced. "How will you do that? You're on the run. And if this magic muddle is messing with you the same as it is everyone else, you won't be functioning properly. Has your magic been misfiring?"

"Let me worry about that. I'll try healing spells on Vorana and see if she'll settle."

I spent the next half hour focused on my dear friend, casting spell after spell over Vorana until she finally fell asleep.

"That helped," Sage said. "But it's temporary."

"Sleep will give her magic the time it needs to rejuvenate," I said. "You stay with her and look after each other."

"Where are you going?"

"Into the basement. I want to look through Zandra's chest of magic. There could be something useful in there. Some of her mother's old books might give us a clue as to what's going wrong with this town." I left Sage lying over Vorana's belly and headed into the basement. It felt like a long time since I'd been here, even though it had only been a few days. I could still smell Zandra in the room, although her scent was fading. Everything good was fading.

I stomped to the magic chest and unlocked it. I pulled out some of the oldest spell books and looked through them. Ancient and illegal dark conjurings were inside the pages, but nothing that would end another's life. I rummaged around, inspecting the potions and powders, looking for anything that could give me an edge over what was happening. I kept drawing blanks.

I hopped out of the chest and went to the corner of the room, where I'd hidden my magic stones behind a loose wall brick.

It took me a few minutes to ease out the brick from the wall. Once extracted, the magic stones pulsed with energy as if they knew I needed them.

Could I do this? Should I even do it? This magic was powerful, but it came at a price.

It had been so long since I'd had all of my ancient demi-goddess magic inside me, and I was uncertain

I'd be able to control it. This may be the time to test that theory. But by doing that, I'd reveal everything to Zandra. She would know who I really was. She could reject me.

I dug out a collar I'd had custom-made to clip my magic stones on. I despised collars, but this one had its uses since I had no pockets. After clipping the stones to the collar, I sealed it around my neck with a spell and headed up the basement steps. Sage sat at the top of the stairs.

I tensed. "Is there a problem with Vorana?"

"She's fine. Sleeping. I wanted to talk to you." Sage's expression was grimly flat. "Do you think what's happening in this town is connected to you?"

I stepped back, wanting to defend myself, but then sighed. "It's not the first time someone has mentioned this to me. And I've had the thought more than once."

"You put a lot of bad guys away. Someone could be out for revenge."

I hesitated. I worried my magic was warping everything, but I much preferred this revenge idea. "I've had powerful werewolves, vampires, and goblins charged with heinous crimes. It could be one of them."

"This trouble feels witchy to me," Sage said.

"I could go through old cases, check with Angel Force to see if any criminals have gotten out on good behavior or escaped," I said, warming to the idea.

"It's possible they're after Zandra. Or you," Sage said. "You haven't told me everything about your past, but I know it's complicated. And I know you have a ridiculous amount of power." She reached forward with a paw and tapped a stone that hung around my neck. "You've kept things hidden for too long, and it's come back to haunt you."

"Let's not get into semantics," I grumbled, wanting to cling to the possibility of a hidden enemy behind all these troubles. "You stay with Vorana. I'll risk going back to Angel Force to see if I can get more information."

Sage shook her head. "Don't think I'll break you out if you get caught. I told Archie and Sammy it was a dumb idea the first time, but they wouldn't listen."

"That dumb idea gave me my freedom."

"For now."

I bid my friend goodbye and left the house with Sammy. We needed to be quick. The morning was fast getting away from us, and a sharp-eyed angel would soon spot us.

"How's Vorana?" Sammy asked.

"Not good," I said.

"What's the plan?"

"As much as it pains me to admit it, I need more help from the angels. And from you."

"I'll do what I can," Sammy said.

"I need you to go inside Angel Force and find Bertoli. He should be back from the hospital by now. We need a list of prisoners I helped arrest who have escaped or gotten out early."

Sammy's eyes widened. "Do you think someone is coming after you?"

"I'm open to all possibilities." Better an old enemy than my misbehaving magic.

He nodded. "You stay out of sight. I'll see what I can do."

I secreted myself in the alleyway opposite Angel Force and waited as Sammy slipped inside the building. It seemed to take an age, but eventually, he emerged with a sheet of paper clamped between his teeth.

He'd just reached me when a wave of fetid magic washed over us. It knocked me off my paws, and I rolled head over tail several times. I felt dizzy and sick as I struggled to get up.

The magic wrapped around me like a sticky web, threatening to strangle me. I hissed and snarled, blasting at the spell with whatever magic came to paw.

I finally got free, coughing and spluttering as I dashed to the alleyway entrance.

I looked around. Sammy was gone.

Chapter 14

All is lost

I stepped out of the alleyway, shaking off the lingering effects of whatever unpleasant magic had rolled through Crimson Cove and knocked me down.

The magic had taken away all sound. There was just silence. Not even a faint breeze stirring or a bird tweeting.

I looked from left to right. There was no sign of Sammy. The paper he'd held in his mouth floated down and landed by my paws. The magic had burned the edges.

Had the spell taken Sammy? Someone or something must have snatched him, since he wouldn't have abandoned me. But why?

I glanced at the Angel Force building, expecting to see a troop of angels racing out to arrest me. No one emerged. They must have bigger problems to deal with than me being on the run.

I called out to Sammy several times and walked along the street, going first one way then the other.

He was gone. I cast a location spell to see where he'd been taken, but it pinged back and whacked me on the head. I growled in frustration then collected the sheet of paper and dashed back to Vorana's house.

I was surprised to find no wards in place, and I could easily gain access. Once inside, I set down the piece of paper on the floor and scanned the list of names. None looked familiar. We hadn't put any of these people away. This list was useless. A dead end.

I hurried up to Vorana's bedroom and nudged open the door with my head. The bed was empty and the covers tossed back.

Perhaps Vorana was in the bathroom. That room was empty, too. There was no sign of her in any of the house's bathrooms, so I dashed down the stairs into the kitchen. She could be feeling better and was making food. The kitchen was deserted.

I scoured each room in turn, but they were all empty. Vorana's purse and shoes sat by the door where she always left them, so she hadn't gone out. And she'd been in no fit state to leave the house. Where had she gone? Wherever it was, she'd taken Sage with her.

An odd, unsettling feeling curled around me. I needed answers, but there was no one around to give them to me.

I left the house and hurried to Sorcha's café. Before I even got to the door, I sensed something was wrong. The lights were off, but the door stood open. I padded inside with caution. The place had an eerie, abandoned feel to it, and a quick search revealed no sign of Sorcha in any of the rooms.

A belching sound came from the kitchen. As I stepped inside, a plate flew at my head then the fridge door slammed open and food sprayed out at me, a cold chunk of cheese thumping me on the behind. Several heads of broccoli and a salami closely followed it.

"Who's doing that? Only cowards hide under magic and throw things."

A cantaloupe melon flew at my head.

"You're not a poltergeist. And this isn't a game." Was that faint laughter?

I hissed at nothing.

Another salami launched at me like a torpedo. I grabbed it between my teeth. At least I could eat this. With dread tingling my toe beans, I ran outside, chewing on my bite of salami, and raced to animal control.

"I thought you'd abandoned us!" Barney stomped out of his office the second he spotted me, Ember clinging to his shoulder. "Where is Zandra? She's late for her shift."

"Of course she is! Don't you know what's going on?"

"Does anybody? If she doesn't show up for her shift in the next ten minutes, she'll lose her job."

I dashed after Barney. "You can't do that. Angel Force is holding Zandra as a suspect in a double murder. Of course, she didn't do it, but I'm working to get her free."

Barney turned, his hands fisted, and his face bright red. "I'm flexible with your workload because you help this town, but my goodwill will only stretch so far. This has gone on for too long. You're taking liberties. You must think I'm an idiot."

"I think the opposite of that! You know how much we respect what you do." Barney had never sounded so angry. "You must understand how unusual this situation is. And I'm sure you know things aren't as they should be in town."

"Watch your backs. We've got a live one!" Glenda Ridgeback and a team member I didn't recognize stumbled in, holding a snarling, writhing sack of something pungent. Acrid smoke slid out of the opening.

"Sedate it and put it outside," Barney said. "All the cages are full to bursting. I need Zandra here. Where is she?"

I hurried along behind Barney. "I just told you!"

There was a gigantic crash from the room containing the penned animals.

"I've got enough to deal with without solving your witch's issues. Tell her if she's not here within the hour, she can find another job."

I stared open-mouthed at Barney as he stomped away.

Randal would help. He loved Zandra. He'd do anything to protect her. I raced to his workstation. All his gadgets and the mess that usually surrounded him were gone.

"If you're looking for Randal, you're too late." Glenda dashed past, wiping green goo off her skintight black jeans. "He left late yesterday."

"He's gone already? I knew he had a new assignment, but I didn't think he'd go without saying goodbye."

"Randal couldn't get out of this place fast enough," Glenda said. "Got to go! Out-of-control critters to bring down and snarl at."

I stepped out of the way as more team members dashed past, almost getting my tail trodden on in their haste.

Who was left to help? Finn had been sidelined for bad behavior. Randal was gone. My misfits were missing or occupied with gathering information, and Vorana and Sorcha had vanished.

It was time to pull out the big magical guns. The Crypt witches might be struggling, but they'd want to protect Zandra. Which reminded me. Where was Abel? He must have returned home. When he realized what a mess this place was, he wouldn't have stuck around. Sensible choice.

I hurried outside, calmed my mind, and threw out a translocation spell to take me to Willow Tree Falls. It was risky, given how wonky the magic was, but it couldn't be avoided. It took half a dozen tries, but the spell finally caught.

My landing was an undignified event in the dirt, face first, whiskers and booping snooter taking the impact. I took a moment to regain my composure and wait for the feeling to return to my face. That spell had felt like it wanted to tear me apart, not transport me.

I struggled to my paws and looked around. It had worked!

Willow Tree Falls was a picturesque village with a rich magical history, built around the large cemetery that sat over the top of a demon prison the Crypt witches had protected for centuries. There was one main street of stores and, beyond that, a dense woodland full of magical creatures and an immensely powerful stone circle that fed the magic users.

It was only as I hurried toward the family home that I noticed how quiet it was. There wasn't a breath of wind nor birdsong. Just silence. Deadly, ominous silence.

I reached the large home where most of the Crypt witches lived. The front door stood open.

"Greetings! It's Juno," I called out to let anyone inside know I was there. It was never wise to creep up on a Crypt witch if you valued your life.

There was no response. Which was odd. There was always someone home.

More dense silence greeted me after I stepped over the threshold. I walked through the entire house. I checked the backyard. Nothing and no one was home.

Perhaps things at the demon prison had gotten so bad they were all there, stopping the prisoners from escaping.

I left the house and hurried toward the cemetery, but I slowed, tensing when there was an ominous boom close by. Pivoting on my paws, I headed to the small street containing most of the shops in Willow Tree Falls.

Smoke billowed out of a store, and as I got closer, my eyes widened. It was Aurora Crypt's store. She ran a magical shop, selling all manner of charms and potions. It was always popular with customers.

Not anymore. The glass at the front was smashed, the door hung off its hinges, and smoke curled out of the openings.

"Aurora, are you in there?" I yelled from the entrance. I squinted through the smoke. There were no signs of life.

Backing up, I peered at the windows above the store where Aurora had a small apartment, although she now lived with her ridiculously wealthy and handsome husband, Lex, in Castle Falls. Smoke poured from the smashed upper floor windows. There was no one up there trying to escape. As I studied all the stores, I saw they were shut, with many windows boarded up, as if the village had prepared for a tornado.

Tempest and Wiggles would help. Apart from my own wonderful witch, Tempest was the strongest of the Crypt witches. She'd still be standing, even if everyone else had fallen.

Cloven Hoof, Tempest's bar, sat on the edge of the village.

I raced away from the smoking store after ensuring there was no one inside. My paws faltered as I drew near to the bar. Just like Aurora's store, someone had trashed it. A blast had removed the main double doors, and a thick, soupy fog rolled out.

Tempest had an apartment above the bar, which she shared with Wiggles, though she spent much of her time at her boyfriend's home. I hoped she hadn't been here when whatever had blown off the front doors arrived.

Picking my way over rubble and broken glass, I carefully avoided injuring my paws as I stepped into the bar. A quiet groan came from the corner of the dance floor.

I hurried toward the noise, a spell primed and ready to throw if anyone attacked. A heap of rubble shifted, and I spotted a small, stubby tail.

"Wiggles!" I raced over to discover Tempest's gassy loyal little hellhound on his side, almost concealed by the debris.

His tail feebly wagged. "Juno? Is that really you, or am I hallucinating again? I thought I saw an ogre just now, but it was mist. And an enormous chunk of cheese has been talking to me for ten minutes. At least, I think it was cheese. It looked like cheese. Smelled amazing."

I crouched beside him. "I came here to get help, but you need it more than I do right now. What happened? Who blew up Cloven Hoof?" I risked a spell to lift the heaviest piece of concrete off him then dug him out using my paws.

Wiggles' eyes flickered closed, and he moaned.

"Stay with me," I urged. "Tell me what happened. Focus on that."

He mumbled a few nonsense words.

"Did you say fire breathers?" I tensed. "Are you saying dragons attacked Willow Tree Falls?"

Wiggles didn't reply.

I tapped him smartly on the side of his muzzle. "Focus! This is important. Are dragons doing this?"

Wiggles sucked in a breath and growled. "Stop hitting me."

"I'll keep hitting with claws out until you answer my question. Was this the work of dragons?"

"No! Smaller. Dangerous. Deadly."

"I can see that. Where is your family?"

He whimpered. "Disappeared."

"Everyone has gone?"

"Can't find them. Tempest. She's gone." The whimpering increased.

"We'll find them all. But first, let's get you healed." Once I'd freed Wiggles from the rubble, I rested my paws on his side but almost jumped back. Some kind of sticky, invisible magic coated him. It was repellent to the touch and made me queasy. It was like the magic I'd removed from Sorcha's freezer.

I spent a moment yanking off all the magic, making sure none lingered, before casting a dozen healing spells. Every spell was a struggle, but with each blast of healing magic, Wiggles became more alert. When I cast the final one, he jerked upright.

His head whipped from side to side. "Where is she?"

"Take a few deep breaths. Compose yourself. Don't panic."

"I'm panicked!" Wiggles snapped his teeth too close to my face. "Tempest is missing. Everyone has gone. What took them?"

I let out a shaky sigh, my nerves fracturing at the possibility the Crypt witches had been defeated, but I had to keep it together. "It's happening in Crimson Cove, too. Zandra is behind bars for murder, and my friends have vanished."

Wiggles jumped up and shook dirt out of his fur. He paced back and forth, his tail twitching in agitation. "Tempest was trying to find Aurora. Her store got blown up."

"I know. It was on fire when I saw it. And when I went to your family home, there was no sign of any Crypt witch. Could they be at the cemetery? That was my next stop."

"Maybe. The demons have been extra evil."

"Talk me through what happened," I said. "Maybe we can see a clue or figure out what's going on if we work together."

Wiggles froze, cocked his head, then nodded. "We went to find Aurora. She wasn't at her store, and the place was destroyed. We went back to the cemetery, and there was no one there. They were all gone. Then we came back here, and bam! Something blasted through the front doors. We tried to fight, but it was chaotic." The words fired out of him. "Magic shooting everywhere. Heat. Power. Gross magic. I couldn't keep up. Neither could Tempest. She went down. I saw her. I tried to get to her, but I was too slow."

"You said fire breathers. What did you mean, if not dragons?"

"Definitely not dragons. Small. Fast-moving. Really powerful. And they'd have to be to mess with us. I've got to find Tempest." Wiggles was moving, but instead of heading for the main doors, he shot up the staircase.

I understood his panic. The prospect of losing your bonded magic user was a heartbreak too grotesque to survive. "I'll help you look."

We spent ten minutes searching the apartment and the bar, but no one was there.

"We should try the cemetery again," I said. "If there are still problems at the prison, we must ensure it's secure, especially if all the Crypt witches have vanished."

Wiggles muttered quietly as he scanned the bar, smoke billowing out of his nose and his eyes gleaming red. "Let's go to the cemetery."

We left the bar, walking close together, scanning the streets for signs of danger.

"When did you first know you were in trouble?" I asked.

"Things have been strange here for a while. Everyone's acting odd. Tempest is still being shady. I didn't want to admit it to anyone, but I was worried about her after we left Crimson Cove."

"Willow Tree Falls feels as distorted as Crimson Cove," I said. "I'm thinking someone is coming after the Crypt witches."

Wiggles' growl was so deep it made my chest hurt. "Anyone who comes for Tempest and her family will be sorry, especially since they were dumb enough to let me live."

We stopped at the cemetery entrance. Powerful protection wards usually guarded the gates, but the large wrought iron black gates stood wide open, and I got no sense of powerful magic protecting the place.

Wiggles growled again. "Something is blocking our ward spells. Normally, the second you get close to the cemetery, you sense them, but they're vibrating as if they're about to break. Their power is muted."

I touched the stone wall and flinched. "It's the same sticky magic I found on you. I found it in Crimson Cove too. We need to get it off. It makes things malfunction."

Wiggles booped his nose against the wall then poked out his tongue. "That feels gross. Let's get to work. If this is covering the prison, everything will break down."

We spent half an hour working around the cemetery, yanking off the sticky, gross magic. As I pulled it off, I sensed the protection wards flare up and cover the prison.

But it was hard, slow, and exhausting work, and it got me no closer to figuring out what was going on in Crimson Cove. However, if the same magic was messing with the Crypt witches and my home, there must be a connection, and I might find it here.

"I think that's it." Wiggles slumped onto his belly as I met him on the other side of the cemetery. "I feel the wards working. Hopefully, we got here in time before any manky old demons slunk out."

I flung off the last of the sticky spell and destroyed it with a blast of magic.

"I need serious snackies after all that work," Wiggles said. "I can't do anything if I'm hungry. My focus will be all over the place."

I smiled to myself. That was more like the Wiggles I knew. If he wasn't thinking about his stomach, something was wrong. "We'll take a ten-minute break to refuel, but then we need to get searching. And we should check the entrance and exits of the prison to make sure nothing got out while the wards were wonky."

As the words left my mouth, darkness slid over the cemetery, blotting out the already weak sun and turning day into a dense, frigid night. An icy fog blew across the cemetery, curling over the top of the wall and landing on top of us. A foul stench accompanied it.

"This is bad." Wiggles scrambled to his paws and looked around.

A low, rumbling growl slid through the fog. "They promised us you would come."

Chapter 15

Demon day

"I do not want to meet whoever just said that." Wiggles stood beside me, snarling softly.

"We may not have a choice," I murmured.

The ground beneath my toe beans shook as whatever underworldly creature drew near. I sparked magic on my paws, ready to strike first.

"You stinking demon better get back in that prison before I find you and bite you," Wiggles said. "I hate your foul taste, but I'll do it. Don't think I won't."

Whatever hid in the fog laughed. "You have no power over us. Not anymore. We have a new master. One more powerful than you."

"Who broke you out of the prison?" I asked.

A spark of red lightning flickered over our heads, and we ducked, expecting it to strike.

"There's more than one of them," Wiggles whispered. "I hear them slithering behind us, too."

"You watch that direction. I'll keep an eye on this one and keep it talking," I murmured. "Show yourself, or are you too afraid? You face two immensely powerful beings. You would be wise to cower at our paws and beg for forgiveness."

"There is nothing to be afraid of in Willow Tree Falls anymore," the deep, disembodied voice said.

"We're here. You should be terrified." A pale haze of blue magic flickered across my paws as the anticipation of battle crept closer.

"They promised us your arrival. So, we waited. A deal was made. It has been fulfilled. We are content."

"Who are you talking about? Who did this deal with you?" I scanned the fog, every shift of shadow threatening violence.

"We came to an arrangement." A demon stepped out of the mist like a shadow unraveling from the night. Its form shimmered between solid and smoke, never quite one or the other, as if reality rejected its presence because it was so unsettling. Swirls of deep violet and black energy coiled around its body, pulsing like a heartbeat.

Its face, if it could be called that, was a shifting mask of darkness, with eyes that glowed like dying stars, flickering between deep crimson and eerie silver. Silver runes etched themselves along its elongated limbs, glowing faintly, shifting and changing. Where it stepped, the ground crackled. Not with fire, but with tiny fractures of shimmering blue light.

"Do you know this one?" I said to Wiggles.

It flicked a glare at the demon. "Maybe. I've captured so many. Demons aren't smart."

"I have been a prisoner for too long. Unfairly prevented from fulfilling my destiny. Not anymore. Not now your power is weakened," it murmured, and I swore the words curled in the air like drifting smoke before fading away. "We have new mistresses."

"Your brain must be addled from spending so long imprisoned by the Crypt witches," I said.

The demon grumbled a low laugh. "I'm free. So are the others. Thanks to them. It is time to repay a debt."

"Are you so weak that you had no choice but to accept their demands?" I asked. "It's pitiful to see such a unique being stooping to the first magic user who tosses them a bone."

"Or they're so powerful the demons had no choice but to accept," Wiggles muttered.

That thought was one I refused to consider.

The demon growled again. "The arrangement was worth it."

I tilted my head. "What did you arrange?"

Wiggles spat out a fireball at whatever approached my back, making me flinch. I trusted Wiggles to deal with any trouble. Providing food didn't distract him, he was a worthy companion.

"It was a simple arrangement." The demon paused, spreading long arms and inhaling deeply as if tasting fresh air after a long spell in a stink bog. "Our freedom for the Crypt Witches' heads. All of them. It was a deal well made."

Wiggles roared his rage and blasted huge bursts of flame in a giant circle that had me leaping to avoid being torched. "Tempest is alive! They're all alive. You haven't destroyed them."

The demon barely flinched. "Little pup. Your fire doesn't bother me. I welcome it."

Wiggle whirled around, facing the demon, his eyes glowing and plumes of smoke drifting from his mouth. "I remember you! Granny Dottie told the story of finding you cowering in an alleyway. You begged for your life. You wanted to be imprisoned because someone had a target on your back. In our prison, you were safe. Pathetic!"

The demon snarled. "I may have been powerless then, but I'm not now. We have waited for this opportunity. We knew it would come. Since you're both bonded to Crypt witches, you cannot live either. Tainted by association."

"Tell me where they are," Wiggles demanded. "I know you haven't killed Tempest."

The demon ignored him and pointed at me. "You, however, we keep alive. At least for now. Our mistresses have a special plan for you. After all, that is why they came."

I stared down the demon, attempting to look strong. I felt anything but. Instead, a weaselly worm of fear took up home in my heart. The chaos inflicted on Crimson Cove and Willow Tree Falls was because of me. The demons wanted me as a gift for whoever controlled them. The Crypt witches, Zandra included, were in danger because of me!

I had to know who was behind this. Who was strong enough to unleash the demons trapped in the prison and control them?

"For once, the famous Juno is lost for words," the demon said. "Your silence amuses me, and I'll be even more amused when you're cringing before me."

"Before you hand me to your new master, at least give me their name, so I know what to prepare myself for."

"And tell me where Tempest is. I'm done playing around." Wiggles blasted out more flame.

The demon roared a laugh as he swatted away the fire. "All in good time, my little pets."

Wiggles slammed his paw into the dirt, and jagged fire swirled around us.

A deafening roar split the air, and from the swirling fog, more demons emerged. Dozens of them, their eyes burning with fire, their clawed hands flexing as they surged toward us.

"Uh-oh. This is more company than I expected," Wiggles said. "I figured most of these douchey demons would run the second they got the chance."

"They must all be a part of this deal to destroy us," I said. "They stay until they achieve their mission."

"Then they'll all fail. I'll be picking demon from between my teeth for weeks after this throw down. Gross."

The rustling of dry leaves signaled more enemies approaching. The air smelled of damp earth and old magic, laced with something acrid and sulfurous. It was a sure sign demons were massing and preparing to strike.

I crouched low, tail flicking as I kept my gaze locked on the hulking figure before me. "Last chance to back off before you make the biggest mistake of your life."

The demon let out a slow, guttural laugh. "You think we fear you?" It tilted its head, eyes gleaming with amusement. "You are outnumbered. Outmatched. This is your end."

I didn't bother responding, just let my magic stir beneath my skin, buzzing, eager to get out. Wiggles stepped forward beside me, a low growl rumbling deep in his chest. He was as ready as I was.

Behind the lead demon, shadows twisted, and the rest of the demon horde emerged from the gloom. Two dozen demons, maybe more. Too many for comfort. Their clawed hands twitched, muscles tensed, ready to pounce.

"Juno," Wiggles muttered, just loud enough for me to hear. "Are we waiting for them to make the first move, or do we skip to the part where we make them regret showing up and threatening our family?"

The demons shifted, their impatience crackling in the air. The leader took a slow step forward then another. Its claws flexed.

We were out of time.

The lead demon lunged faster than I expected. I barely had time to react before it was on me, claws swiping for my throat. Instinct took over. I twisted, using its momentum against it, and slammed my paws onto its chest. We hit the ground, a snarl ripping from the demon's throat as it writhed beneath me, trying to throw me off. My claws dug in, magic humming in my murder mittens.

It bucked once, nearly unseating me, but I held firm. Wiggles was at my side, his body tensed, flames licking out of his mouth. "You need a helping paw?"

"No, just watch the others. If we bring this one down, it might make them wary. They could back off."

The other demons hesitated, watching their leader struggle with me. But their indecision wouldn't last long, so I had to act quickly.

I jumped back as the demon slashed at my belly and flung a pulse of shimmering energy at its face. The force sent it skidding across the dirt. But I had no time to celebrate. The others were moving.

Wiggles let loose a furious howl, his paws slamming into the ground again. A shockwave of flame rippled out, sending the first wave of demons sprawling. But they were resilient, climbing back to their feet with inhuman speed.

A pair of demons lunged at me. I darted aside, flipping into a roll before springing up, claws glowing with power. With a swipe of my murder mittens, I slashed the air, sending an arc of magic that struck them in the chests. They howled as they stumbled back, their dark forms flickering like smoke.

"Watch your left!" Wiggles yelped.

I spun just in time to see another demon diving for me, its teeth bared, its clawed hands reaching for me. It was too close. My heart lurched.

Then Wiggles was there, ramming into its side like an unstoppable force. The demon was sent flying, slamming into a twisted tree with a sickening crunch. It didn't get up.

"I appreciate the save," I said.

"Anytime. Try not to get eaten or incinerated! I can't do this alone." Wiggles launched himself into another demon, his fangs crackling with fire.

A giant of a demon lifted its clawed hand toward me, a swirling black vortex forming in its palm.

I threw a blast of energy, but the demon deflected it with a flick of its claws then hurled the vortex at me. I dodged, but the edge of the magic grazed my side, sending a jolt of freezing pain through me. My vision blurred, and I stumbled.

That was a mistake.

The demon lunged, claws aiming for my face.

Wiggles roared, and a wall of fire erupted between us, forcing the demon back with a sickening screech.

I forced myself to move. No more mistakes. My magic had to do my bidding. I was done being cautious and worrying if it would serve me. It had done my bidding for millennia, and it would do so again.

I slipped off my collar and slammed my paws against a stone. A sphere of blinding light erupted from it, sending a shockwave that rippled through the cemetery. Demons staggered, some collapsing under the force.

I locked eyes with the vortex-conjuring giant demon and unleashed more magic. A column of searing energy burst from my outstretched paw, colliding with the demon in an explosion of light. Its body writhed as I jumped on it and took it down.

The remaining demons hesitated as they witnessed my ancient magic swirling around them. Magic they had probably only heard of in whispered stories of myth and legend. And I was a legend. They now knew who they were messing with.

I pinned the demon, snarling in its face. It was weak. Almost on its last breath. And yet, it still found the energy to laugh at me.

"You have lost," it slurred. "Everything you love has been taken from you, as it should be. You are defeated. You just don't know it yet."

I slashed my glowing claws across the foul creature's face. "Tell me who controls you. I must know."

The demon let out a final, ragged breath and disintegrated beneath my paws, leaving behind a pile of ash and a veil of smoke.

Wiggles took command, stepping forward, fire licking at his paws. "Back into the prison. Now. Unless you want to end up like that."

There were growls and snarls, but not a single demon had any fight left in them. Instead, they shifted and hunched, not looking at me. The air tasted of fear and uncertainty.

"Don't make me tell you again," Wiggles said.

One by one, the demons melted away, their forms flickering and vanishing as they slid into the prison.

I exhaled, my legs shaking as I met Wiggles' gaze.

He huffed. "I hate demons. Stinking dirtbags."

I snorted, shaking out my fur. "You and me both."

Wiggles cocked his head. "What was that magic you used? It sure got the demons' attention."

"Something old." I wiped demon ash off my paws.

"And weird. You've got power in those fancy stones on your collar." Wiggles went to sniff the collar, but I swiped it away and reattached it around my neck.

"That's not for you. It isn't safe."

His eyes narrowed. "I have power."

"But I'm older than you. That makes me wiser. Wise enough to know my limits. And yours."

"I got no limits."

"We all have limits."

Wiggles grunted. "I'll go check how these dirtbags are behaving. See if any need you to smite them with your old weird magic."

I settled in the dirt, resting as I felt my way into this extra power. It was an odd feeling to regain some of what I'd lost so long ago. Odd but familiar.

"That's the last of them settled back in their cells. Good little demons." Wiggles returned to join me. "Did you get the answers you needed before that stinky demon went up in ash and smoke?"

"It refused to tell me anything useful." I scowled at the pile of ash beside me.

"Lousy sneaks. Someone must know where Tempest is. I will find her, even if I have to interrogate every one of those suckers."

A high-pitched squeal split the air. A demon materialized, its twisted form writhing in the dim light. It danced around us, dodging Wiggles' fireballs.

"You have lost. You have lost," it taunted. "The trio will not be defeated. They will free us, and we will win."

A familiar, eerie sensation prickled down my spine, like icy fingers trailing across my fur. I glanced around. "The trio. Are they here?"

"Answer Juno," Wiggles growled, stomping on the end of the demon's tail.

The demon laughed maniacally. "You don't have enough power to stop them. They're our masters. They will soon rule all. Your magic is nothing to them. They laugh at you. We all laugh."

"If they send a horde of demons instead of facing us themselves, they must be afraid of us," I said.

"And if they aren't, they should be," Wiggles said.

I scanned the darkened cemetery. Was this mysterious trio watching us? "Take us to them."

"You aren't worthy to stand in their presence," the demon hissed. "Such greatness. If you ever saw them, you would wither and grovel on your knees, puny magic users."

"This jerk is getting on my nerves," Wiggles muttered. "Let me smoke it."

"We need to keep it alive," I said. "It knows who's behind this. We have to keep it talking."

Wiggles grabbed the demon by the scruff of its neck and shook it. "Tell us who's done this to Willow Tree Falls. Who's messing with our magic? And where is Tempest?"

The demon only laughed harder. Then, with a flick of its clawed hand, it engulfed itself in a shower of dark sparks and disintegrated.

"What the—" Wiggles stepped back, shaking hot ash from his fur.

"I thought you said you got them all?" I stared at the pile of smoking ash.

Wiggles grunted. "Even you make mistakes."

I shrugged. "Rarely. What did it mean, the trio? Is that who's controlling them?"

"We'll never know. It destroyed itself to avoid telling us anything. And now I stink of gross demon ash. Tempest will make me take a bath."

"Whoever is controlling these demons has the power to make them do anything. Fight us. Destroy Willow Tree Fall. Even make them self-destruct."

"That's some serious power." Wiggles exhaled a puff of smoke, glancing warily around the cemetery. "That was definitely the last one, right?"

"You know more about demons than I do," I admitted. "But I sense something out there. Not a demon but something watching. Do you feel it?"

"I don't know. My stomach is growling so loud I can barely hear you. All that fighting made me starving. Now the demons are under control, let's go grab a mountain of fuel."

A dense swirl of smoke drifted toward us. The moment it reached my booping snooter, I gagged. I knew that smell, but where had I experienced it before?

"Not just yet. Something is coming."

"Over there," Wiggles growled, also on the alert. "It just moved outside the cemetery gates."

"Another demon?" I whispered.

"I didn't get a good enough look. Could that be what you're sensing?"

"Let's go see," I said.

Wiggles hesitated. "I can't leave the cemetery unguarded. The magic wards are holding, but this place is unstable. I've got to make sure the demons can't get out."

"Then stay here. I've got this." I dashed toward the cemetery gates and onto the road.

Inhaling deeply, I caught that same pungent odor, and this time, I remembered where I'd smelled it before. It was the same stench I'd inhaled when I'd uncovered Erick Farten's killer, Sylvia.

Was Sylvia connected to all of this? Had we underestimated her power? No. It couldn't be her. She was locked up, and there was no way she'd be orchestrating this chaos from inside a cell.

Unless... Sylvia wasn't working alone. Or had she escaped and Angel Force didn't know?

The demon had spoken of a trio. Had we only caught one, while two more remained free?

I spent ten minutes searching the street, looking for the source of that smoky stink, but it had vanished. So had the sensation of being watched. That nasty, icy trickle of unease rattling down my spine. Whatever had lurked in the shadows was gone.

For now.

But this fight wasn't over, and I knew now this problem had emerged from my past and was destroying everything I loved.

Why? Revenge? Jealousy? Spite?

I didn't know. But whatever the reason, my past would not destroy my present. And one thing I knew with an unshakeable surety, no matter the challenge or obstacle, magical misfits never gave up.

Chapter 16

The trio

"Let me know when you find Tempest." I stood with Wiggles outside the now secure gates of the cemetery.

"It feels so weird that my witch has disappeared. I'm usually the one who goes off on an adventure." Wiggles puffed out a perfect circle of smoke. "Not so much now I have the pups. It's tough having responsibilities, but those pups sure are fun."

"Sadly, I don't think Tempest is off having a fun adventure. The Crypt witches are in serious trouble, and it's down to us to fix this."

Wiggles looked around, growling softly. "I'm not known for being the responsible one, but I can adjust."

"Sometimes we're all forced into roles we'd rather not be in," I said.

"What's the role you don't want to take on?" Wiggles asked.

"Truth teller." I'd been hiding things from Zandra for too long. But once I got her free and her name

188

cleared, everything would change. And I meant that in every sense of the word.

I gently booped my nose against Wiggles, inhaling his sulfury stink. A part of me didn't want to leave Willow Tree Falls. At least here, I had Wiggles for support. But I needed to get back to Crimson Cove. The chaos wouldn't stop just because I'd left town.

"Don't go getting yourself killed," Wiggles said.

"Same to you."

"That's impossible, But I appreciate the concern."

We said our goodbyes, and I cast a translocation spell. Nothing happened. I tried again and got the same result. That shouldn't happen. Not with a portion of my original magic spinning through me.

"Let me give you a boost," Wiggles said. "I don't seem too badly affected by all this misfiring magic. Although I am way gassier, but that could be the old bean and cheese burrito I ate from the trash just before Cloven Hoof was attacked." He huffed hot, sour smoke over me, and I cast the spell again. It resisted but finally took.

The magic dumped me back in Crimson Cove, flat on my belly and limbs splayed. It was such an undignified and unnatural landing for one with such perfect balance and poise.

I rolled over and shook out my fur. I'd made it back in one piece, but I wouldn't try that spell again anytime soon.

I looked around the street where I'd landed. It was deserted. Crimson Cove looked like a ghost town. I may be alone, but I was determined.

As unhappy as I was to acknowledge I was the source of these troubles, if it was true, the solution lay within me. I had to get to the bottom of the identification of the trio. What power was so all-consuming and dominant that it cowed an entire prison full of demons and bent them to their will?

Whatever it was, I needed to see Zandra and make sure she was safe in her cell. And if any angel dared to stop me, they'd regret it.

The former buzz surrounding the Angel Force building was gone. As I approached the main doors, not a single angel had flown in or out. In fact, the front doors were wide open.

I paused by the entrance as worry scurried down my tail like an impudent rodent.

The reception area was empty, as was the large open-plan office where most of the angels congregated to gossip, eat donuts, and occasionally work.

I looked in Cythera's office. Papers had been discarded, and her chair was shoved back against one wall, suggesting she'd left in a hurry.

With all the angels gone, it would be easier to get Zandra out of her cell. I hurried to the door leading to the cells and found it open. I shoved my way through and dashed along the corridor.

Each cell door was also open. No one was inside. I checked every single cell. They were all empty. Zandra was gone.

A noise from the open-plan office had me jumping around and tensing. I snuck back along the corridor and peeped around the side of the door.

Finn mooched about, looking more demon than angel. Dark flecks of magic sparked across his wings, and his eyes glowed an otherworldly shade of red.

His head whipped around as he sensed me watching him, and he snarled.

"Finn, it's me!" I stepped cautiously into the office. "Where is everybody?"

The light in his eyes faded, and he shook his head. "Ugh! Sorry. Gross demon issues. They're all gone."

"Have you seen Zandra? Did the prisoners get set free, or did they escape?"

He puffed out his chest. "You can thank me for that."

"What did you do?"

"I got here and found the place abandoned, other than the prisoners. It seemed cruel to leave them in there with no one feeding them or checking their wellbeing, so I flipped the switch, dropped the magic wards, and let them go with a full pardon." Finn chuckled.

I hissed. "Zandra's life is at risk. She was safer behind bars. Bertoli was watching her."

"That's news to me. Since when have you been such close friends with Bertoli? He's way too uptight."

"Why are you even here?" I asked. "I thought you'd been suspended."

"Pah! There's no one here to tell me what I should do. If I want to work, I will. If I want to set everyone free, I'll do that, too. A few more chaos makers on the streets will make things more exciting."

This wasn't the Finn I knew and adored, so I needed to tread carefully to avoid him going full demon. "Where did Zandra go?"

Finn shrugged as he sniffed an abandoned plate of cake and then tossed it across the room. "I couldn't tell you. All I know is she didn't hang around once the door opened."

"Zandra didn't stop to see how you were doing?"

"Why would she? I'm great. Perfectomundo."

I hopped on a desk and batted at Finn's wing to keep his attention on me for more than a few seconds. "Zandra is in trouble. Someone wants her dead."

"I don't see that being a problem. We all die eventually," Finn said. "Although angels live a long time, I imagine you will too, with all that magic whizzing around you. And what have you got around your neck?" He reached for the collar containing my remaining enchanted stones, but I batted away his hand. "Focus on Zandra!"

He shrugged again. "As you said, I've been suspended. If she's in danger, I can't do anything to help. I'd only make things worse. Might even end up getting her killed. Might even kill her."

"Don't talk like that. You may not work for Angel Force at the moment, but you're still her friend," I said. "You should care. Stop that demon from talking on your behalf and help me."

Finn snarled but drew in a deep breath and shook out his wings, dark sparks flying everywhere.

I wasn't sure if he'd gained any control by doing that, but I pressed on. "Agatha and Thelma were murdered by mistake. From the back view, they looked like Zandra."

"Cute? Zandra has a great rear end."

I slashed at him. "Someone wants my witch dead."

Finn's gaze narrowed. "Bad luck for them. They failed."

"Don't you see? By letting Zandra go, you've put her at risk. She was safest here, hidden in a cell behind magic wards."

"Doubtful. The last time I saw Cythera, she was fighting Bertoli because she thought he'd stolen her paper clips. Anyone with enough cunning could have slipped in and done what they liked to Zandra."

"Not while she was behind wards," I said. "And where's Bertoli? Was he injured in the fight?"

"Beats me. Everyone's gone. We've been abandoned. The only person you can rely upon is yourself. Do that and you'll have no worries."

"I refuse to believe that," I said. "There's goodness in everyone, even though it gets buried deep, and they forget how to use it. Even you, in your current form."

Finn chuckled. "I appreciate you believing in me, but my demon is a douche. Don't waste your time on me."

"I never give up on a friend in trouble. Will you help me find Zandra?"

His gaze grew unfocused. "You shouldn't be around me. I'm not safe. I'm losing control, and there's nothing I can do about it. I want to help, but you wouldn't want me hanging around you for too long."

I appreciated Finn's honesty, but I needed a friend right now. "Are there any angels left in Crimson Cove who could help?"

"Do angels ever really help? We poke our noses in, hand out fines, and tell people off. You're on your own," Finn said. "Oh, hey. Here's an idea. Try the hospital. If Zandra got out and found herself in trouble, she could be hurt."

That thought was as appealing as stale kibble, but it gave me something to focus on.

I left Finn to his aimless mooching and random acts of destruction and dashed out of Angel Force. The streets were empty. No people around. They were most likely hiding or out, causing chaos. I slowed to put out a fire in a house but then continued toward the hospital.

I tugged on my bond with Zandra, relieved to find it, but it was weak. Did that mean she'd been hurt? Was I losing her? Or was her magic distorted by whatever was affecting this town, changing her in ways I couldn't understand?

What would happen if I lost my witch for good?

When we'd first connected, I'd convinced myself this would be a temporary bond. I had a destiny to fulfill. I always believed I'd get back my demi-goddess powers. I'd return to my old form, my old ways. The plan had been to reclaim my powers, to have my adoring subjects back, my glorious homes, and all the wealth I desired.

But I didn't want that anymore.

My bond with Zandra ran deep. It meant everything to me. And I only realized it now, on the verge of losing her and everything we'd built together.

It all felt meaningless without Zandra. I had to ensure she was safe. Then all cards would be strewn across the table. No more secrets.

I arrived at the hospital and hurried inside, not caring if a nurse reprimanded me for shedding fur in places I shouldn't. Hygiene be damned!

The place still functioned, though there was an air of desperate panic as nurses and doctors dashed around. It took several minutes before I got someone to stop and pay me attention.

"I'm looking for Zandra Crypt," I said.

"Check the desk," the nurse I'd stopped said before rushing away. "We've got more patients here than we know what to do with. If the injury isn't critical, they're being turned away. You should hope she's not here."

I asked a few more people, but they ignored me as they dashed about.

Frustrated, I abandoned my attempts to get sense out of anyone and searched each room.

It was a small hospital. Magic healed most minor ailments and injuries, so there weren't many rooms to check. I completed my search of the private rooms and treatment areas on one level then headed upstairs.

I discovered a patient sitting up in bed. It was Charlie Victor. I'd recognize that ginger beard anywhere. He was friends with Randal Nix and had visited Crimson Cove with Eric Farten.

Eric had come to an unfortunate end, being scared to death, quite literally. Charlie had almost met the same fate and been stuck in a magical coma since the attack.

He glanced over as I stood in the doorway and clutched at his bedsheets. "What are you doing here?"

"Looking for a friend," I said. "You won't remember me. I'm Juno. I assisted Angel Force with their investigation into Erick's murder."

"Oh. I didn't know that." He jumped as something was knocked over in the corridor. "I want to leave. Things are weird here."

"Things are strange everywhere in town," I said. "How long have you been awake?"

He shrank back as I grew closer. "Two days. I'm still catching up. Processing, you know. I don't suppose you know Randal Nix, do you? I was hoping he'd visit and help me."

"Of course, we're friends. We work together at animal control," I said. "Well, we did. Randal left town recently. He got a new assignment."

"He hasn't been to see me," Charlie said. "I thought he'd want to know how I was doing."

"He stopped by most days. He was worried about you."

"I don't remember. And no one is saying much, other than I need to stay here." Charlie twisted his fingers into his beard.

"I'm sorry about what happened to Erick," I said. "Do you remember much about the night he died?"

"Yeah. Most of it. That was a lousy way to die," Charlie said.

"Were you good friends?"

"Not that close. I only spent time with Erick because Randal liked him, and we always did things as a trio. It was easier to keep quiet about his annoying habits than rock the boat. But Erick was always sniffing and had a gross dripping nose. He blamed allergies. I don't know. I think he did it to annoy me."

That word again. Trio. A trio of troublesome magic users were behind this spiraling situation.

"Tell me about that night?" I asked.

Charlie's eyes narrowed. "Why are you asking about it?"

"I'm still investigating the case. There are a few loose ends. We caught Erick's killer, Sylvia, but something still felt wrong. Unfinished." I crouched, planning to hop onto the end of the comfortable bed.

"Stop! Don't come any closer!"

I froze. "Why not? I'm no threat."

"I've gone off cats."

"We're magnificent. Every household should have at least a dozen."

"Not mine."

"Has a cat done you wrong in the past?"

Charlie's expression grew conflicted. "I know you said you caught Erick's killer, but I think you're wrong."

"Did you see who murdered him?" I asked. "It wasn't Sylvia?"

"Of course I saw! We were in the kitchen stocking up on snacks when there was this scratching at the back door. Erick went outside to see what it was."

"What did he find?"

"He'd been gone a while, so I checked on him and saw him running across the backyard."

"Was someone chasing him?"

"Three cats, black and fiery. They're what put me in the hospital and murdered Erick, not Sylvia."

My heart pounded. "Three black cats. Small?"

"Yeah. Kittens. How did you know how big they were? Did you tell them to hunt us?"

I ignored the foolish question. "And fire breathers?"

"That's right. I don't know what problem they had with Erick, but they took him down and then stood around his body as if they were having a friendly chat. One even jumped up and down on him like he was a trampoline. I yelled at them, and that's when they whacked me with a spell, too. It flew toward me in a wave. I couldn't get away."

I could barely breathe as I sank onto my belly, not believing what I'd heard. The three adorable foster kittens we'd been living with all this time. They were the trio.

Chapter 17

The truth is out

"Are you okay?" Charlie peered down at me from his bed.

"No. I'm very much the opposite of okay. Are you sure it was three small black kittens who attacked you?" I jumped on Charlie's bed, causing him to squeak and cower.

"Positive. I did a double-take when I saw what chased Erick. He's not into running, but I've never seen him run like that before. I was about to tease him, but then I saw the terror on his face. He kept looking over his shoulder and squealing. That's when I knew those kittens weren't messing about."

"Did Erick do something to them? There must have been a reason they attacked." This had to be wrong. The kittens weren't causing all this chaos. Three tiny fluff babies would never have so much malevolence.

"Nothing! He just went outside to see what that noise was. They scratched at the door. They wanted him to go outside so they could attack." Charlie jerked his leg away when I pressed a paw against it.

"Did they say anything?" The kittens didn't speak much beyond hisses and meows. They had yet to come into their voices.

"Not a word. They just attacked. They must have come to Randal's house for a reason, though. I don't think it was bad luck we got picked on."

"Randal's house! Of course," I said. "Could they have mistaken Erick for Randal?"

"They didn't explain the method behind their madness," Charlie said. "One minute they were chasing down Erick, and the next, they whacked him with nasty magic. Flames flickered out of them while they ran, and their forms kept shifting. I'd blink, and they'd look like something else, and then they'd be back to kittens."

"What did they turn into?" I asked.

"Misty shapes. Tall like a person, but also not. I thought my eyes were deceiving me or it was a trick of the light, but it kept happening. It was only when they knocked Erick off his feet that I knew this wasn't a game."

"You said they stood around Erick's body after they brought him down. Was it to make sure they'd killed him?"

"They did something in the dirt. Scratching at it or digging a hole. I couldn't see for sure because it was so dark. I wondered if they were going to bury him, hide the evidence, you know."

"Or write something," I said. "Someone scratched a word into the dirt and hid it beneath Erick's body."

"The angel who came to see me told me they had a suspect for a while because of that name. Tempest, was it?"

"That's right, but we swiftly discounted her," I said. "If the kittens wrote her name, they must have been trying to frame Tempest. But why do that?"

"You're asking me?"

"I'm putting the question out there to the universe," I said. "Tempest is a Crypt witch, and the kittens were obsessed with her when she visited Crimson Cove. They wouldn't leave her alone. Even when she returned home, they visited. I assumed her power drew them to her."

"Is that why things are being so strange? These kittens are taking the Crypt witch's power and channeling it?"

"I... perhaps. But again, why? They're kittens. They have power, but it's still evolving. Are they really behind all this chaos?"

"I have no answers to these questions," Charlie said.

I fixed him with a stern expression. "It was definitely three small black kittens?"

"Yes! It happened fast, but I'm not making any of this up."

"If they're stealing magic, then they're getting stronger every day. Some magic users absorb another's power, but they're rare and extremely unpopular," I said.

"That's no shocker. Who would want to be around someone who takes your abilities?" Charlie said. "I'm glad I'm into all the tech stuff. It's not so popular."

"It was popular enough for the kittens to hunt you and your friends."

Charlie gulped. "Do you think they'll come back for me?"

I regarded him steadily. "I don't think so. They sought out Randal's house. Maybe they wanted Randal dead, but you got in the way."

"Why? Randal's a good guy."

I didn't like where my thoughts were tugging me, but I had to acknowledge the issue. "Because of Randal's connection to Zandra, my wonderful witch. They wanted to frame Tempest and drive a wedge between the sisters. They planned to bring down a powerful Crypt witch, shatter the family dynamic, and make everyone vulnerable."

"Don't the Crypt witches have something to do with demons?" Charlie asked. "Are the kittens really demons?"

"They do. And I don't think so. I never got a hint of demon energy when they misbehaved. But the Crypt witches are in trouble. Their demon prison is in chaos. I've just been helping round up the escapees."

"Are you sure the kittens aren't demons in disguise? It would make sense. They want to get their friends out of the cells."

"They're troublemakers, but I considered it youthful exuberance. You know what magical youngsters are like."

"Not really. I don't have a family of my own," Charlie said.

"Why would the kittens want to mess with the Crypt witches?" I mused. "That's what I need to find out. Have you seen the kittens recently?"

"No! And I don't want to. I never want those tiny, evil critters anywhere near me. And you should avoid them too. If they can take down a Crypt witch, then they can deal with you."

"I may be small, but I'm mighty."

There was another crash in the corridor, and Charlie jerked in his bed. "Is it safe to stay here?"

"Most likely not, although it's one of the least chaotic places in town. If you're well enough, I suggest you leave immediately. Get as far away from here as you can. Don't return to Randal's house to collect your belongings. Just go."

"The doctors want to keep me under observation for forty-eight hours. I was out for over a month, so they want to make sure everything works right."

"The magic whacked you hard," I said. "I suspect the kittens didn't want to leave behind any witnesses. You weren't supposed to survive that attack."

"They failed to kill me." Charlie gulped. "I'm still vulnerable, aren't I?"

"So long as you get out as quickly as you can, you'll be fine." I hopped off the bed and hurried to the door, a dozen questions swirling in my head.

"Wait, you're leaving?" Charlie asked. "Shouldn't I get protection? Can you protect me with your small but mighty magic?"

"You can get yourself out of town without me," I said. "Be quiet, stealthy, and cautious. Don't draw any attention to yourself."

"What will you do?"

"Hunt those kittens." I hurried into the corridor, hopping over a tray of fallen medicines and dodging past several abandoned wheelchairs before I made it to the exit. Charlie seemed so certain the kittens were behind this chaos, but I struggled to accept that possibility. I'd never allow such danger close to Zandra.

Had Charlie gotten muddled because of the spell that whacked him? Being stuck in a magical coma for any length of time would do a person no good. Could he have dreamed the kittens were involved?

Perhaps he saw them just before the attack on Erick, confusing his memories. But he'd seemed so certain they were behind this.

I had to talk to them and get the truth.

The first stop on my magical kitten hunt was Vorana's house. They hadn't been there the last time I'd dropped by, but I needed to check their regular haunts. I headed into the backyard and stopped by the shed. I'd found Sage here, bound and struggling, hit by nasty magic.

Had that been the kittens? They always picked on her. Did they consider Sage a threat, or did they want her out of the way so they'd have access to Vorana and the house with no one monitoring them?

I looked over my shoulder. Things had been going wrong inside the house. Appliances kept breaking. Objects kept going missing. And Vorana had been exhausted for weeks, as had Sage. Was that the kittens' doing? Were they absorbing or stealing Vorana and Sage's energy and using it to get stronger?

Sage had power, but Vorana's magic was connected to her love of literature. She'd always been a delightfully bookish witch and enjoyed studying obscure texts about magic. Had the kittens wanted access to her knowledge, so they took it?

I gasped. The tiny red pinpricks on Vorana's arm. Had the kittens been biting her, sinking their tiny claws and teeth into her skin and draining her of knowledge and power? Those marks were about the right size for needle-teeth kitten bites.

But what was their motive? They were just magical kittens. Powerful, but not bad.

After searching the house and finding no sign of the kittens, I headed into town. I needed to search swiftly. Darkness was descending, and with Crimson Cove so unstable, I didn't want to be out alone for long. Not that I couldn't handle trouble. I had more power simmering inside me than I'd had for a long time. But I wasn't sure I could rely on it. I needed to test it.

I focused on the kittens and threw out a location spell. It swirled around me, lifted me off my paws, and dumped me on my head.

"That was unnecessary," I muttered as I shook out my fur. "Show me where those wretched kittens are. I need to talk to them."

I tried twice more, and each time, I was swept off my paws and rolled around most unceremoniously.

A light laughter hit my ears. I was instantly on the alert.

"What fun you are having by yourself, my delicious fluffy one." Remus Salamander stepped out of the shadows, dressed head to toe in pale pink with a matching top hat. He carried his silver-tipped cane in one hand.

"Greetings. I'm having a few issues with my magic," I said.

"If the rumors ring true, so is everybody else."

"I'm trying to locate three missing kittens most urgently, but the location spell won't work."

"I've been hearing about the fun and games residents have been having while I slumber," Remus said. He displayed too much fang as he smiled. "I was considering bringing my vampires to town to play."

"I wouldn't do that," I said. "The town has enough trouble, and your hive is struggling to control itself."

"Are we now? Or are we doing what comes naturally? You should be careful. You look delicious."

"No eating me! I'm too busy to fight you."

Remus snarled and reached down to grab me, but I shot out a vicious spell, which actually worked, causing him to recoil and hiss.

"You displease me," Remus said.

"And you infuriate me. I'm not in the mood to negotiate whether I should be your snack," I said. "You help, or you leave."

"Will you feed me afterward?"

"I won't stake you through the heart. How's that for a deal?"

Remus laughed again, the sound a sharp scrape against my ear. "I see you aren't in the mood for pleasantries."

"I'm in the mood for fixing this town, finding my witch, and learning if the kittens we've been looking after are behind this."

"Kittens... they make a particularly delicious snack."

"Remus, focus. And never mention feeding on kittens again, or we won't be friends." I slashed a murder mitten against his calf to sharpen his focus. "I know Oak Park Ridge suffers, much like Crimson Cove. You should want to help."

"We are experiencing some... difficulties. There is a touch of feeding frenzy in the air." Remus glowered down at me then inspected his torn pants.

"I've discovered a mysterious trio is behind all of this. It's possible that the trio are the three foster kittens we've been looking after at Vorana's house."

"Tiny kittens are causing this bedlam? I don't think so."

"Walk with me. I'm looking for them, and I have no time to waste." I strode off.

Remus soon joined me, his cane tapping lightly on the road. "May I eat them if I find them?"

"No. Well, I'll think about it. They're messing with Zandra, so that means the rules get bent."

"I enjoy rule bending. Tell me why you believe these tiny bundles of nothingness are causing such trouble."

"I'm working through that, but I went to the hospital to find Zandra and met a patient who told me the kittens attacked him and killed his friend."

Remus looked skeptical.

"I didn't believe it at first, but he's on to something. Those kittens were obsessed with Tempest. And Tempest and Zandra's Granny Dottie recognized they have an unusual power."

"Some creatures can be powerful. You're a fine example. And you have a little something extra about you. What have you been juicing on?" Remus bent to pet me, but I shied away. I didn't trust him not to take a sneaky drink.

"Let's focus on the kittens," I said. "While they've been at Vorana's, things have been going wrong."

"Such as?"

"Electrical faults. Vorana's been excessively tired, and Sage was bound and trapped in the shed. She didn't remember who did it, but what if it was the kittens?"

"Sage can be grumpy," Remus said. "Perhaps she offended someone, and they took their revenge."

"I'm not finished. Sorcha was the first person to foster the kittens, but she quickly handed them over because she couldn't cope. She tried again but had to give them back to me because she couldn't manage their power."

"That is odd," Remus said. "Sorcha handles many disaffected, cranky, and downright mean creatures. She enjoys a challenge."

"Exactly. If Sorcha couldn't handle those kittens, then it shows there's something different about them. And recently, things have been going wrong in her café, too."

"They held a grudge because she wouldn't look after them?"

"What if the kittens are testing their limits? Trying out different magic," I said.

"Trying it out on the whole town, it would appear." Remus gestured at the remains of a smoldering house.

"They're refining their skills," I said. "And it's spread across Crimson Cove and into Oak Park Ridge."

"My vampires are immune to such trickery."

"Not according to Archie," I said. "He's avoiding you. He said your vampires keep trying to bite him. You included."

Remus snarled then looked shamefaced. "There have been a few incidents, but it's just boisterous play."

"You haven't heard the best bit," I said. "When Tempest came to town, the kittens tried to frame her for Erick Farten's murder."

"I don't know him."

"He was Randal's friend. I think they meant to murder Randal."

"The charming tech mage who has a crush on Zandra?" Remus asked.

"Yes! They went to the house with a target in mind but got the wrong person."

"Why do that?"

"Bringing down Tempest messes with the Crypt Witch coven," I said. "And killing someone Zandra is fond of would cause a rift between Tempest and Zandra, further destabilizing the Crypt witches."

"A powerful coven at war would have devastating consequences," Remus said.

"Their attempts failed, but only just," I said. "And they're not finished yet. Zandra escaped from her cell and is missing, as are some of my friends. Vorana and Sage have vanished. And when I was with Sammy, we were trying to get information from Angel Force, and magic whacked into us. Sammy disappeared!"

"Are the kittens destroying the people you love?" Remus shook himself as if removing an oversized overcoat.

"I... yes, they could be. I learned information from the demons who escaped from the Crypt witch prison. A deal was struck. It involved destroying everything I love."

Remus exhaled softly. "For that, I am sorry. I sense something is wrong, something deeply troubling. And I wish I could help, but I have an almost insatiable desire to feed from you, so I shouldn't be here."

"I don't take it personally," I said. "You should be with your hive. Stay inside. Resist temptation. All of this is connected, and I must stop it."

"How do you intend to do that without support?"

I shook my head, jangling the stones around my neck. "I have a few ideas. Go home. Lock the doors. Try not to feed from anything or anyone that isn't willing."

Remus snarled at me but then vanished, leaving nothing but a waft of smoke.

I looked around the eerily deserted town, resolute in what I needed to do. The more pieces I put together, the more obvious it seemed. The adorable kittens I'd grown fond of were behind this.

Whatever was hiding inside those innocent forms, I needed to dig it out and destroy it.

But with my magic not operating at full power, I needed more help. And since my friends were in trouble or missing, I had to turn inward for that help.

I unclipped my collar, removed two stones, and set them on the ground. I reattached the collar and stepped back, staring at the stones. It wasn't all of my power, but most of it. I needed to draw on something as old, twisted, and unyielding as the kittens were using.

I stepped on the magic stones. The power inside them curled around me, forming a giant bowl of light. It lifted me off my paws, twirling me around and around until I was dizzy and couldn't see straight. The power flipped me upside down a few times, but it kept coming, feeding me as I absorbed it.

It felt like too much power. I couldn't keep taking it, but it was mine, so I needed to accept it. This town, and everyone I held dear, was relying on me.

Just as I felt I couldn't spin anymore, I was dropped onto the ground and landed on my belly. I kept my eyes closed and drew in deep breaths. Power tingled through me like a live wire. Had I always been this strong? How would I control such energy?

The sensations were overwhelming, and I must have blacked out for a few minutes because I suddenly jerked awake as a cold mist drifted over me, laughter haunting my ears.

"Welcome back, Juno. We finally convinced you to stop hiding. It has been too long."

Chapter 18

End game

"Who's there?" I staggered to my paws. The magic I'd absorbed with such speed made me shaky and light-headed. I wasn't used to it.

"I'm offended you don't remember us." A croaky female voice drifted around me, making it hard to determine the source.

"If you show your face, that would be helpful," I said. "Only cowards hide in the shadows."

"We've been showing a version of our faces for some time, yet you refused to acknowledge us. Was that ignorance or stupidity?" That was a different voice. Lighter, yet cold.

The power I'd absorbed took its time to settle, leaving me shivery and uncertain I could trust it. Did I have enough magic to go up against this mysterious trio? Was I about to find out the kittens had been deceiving me all this time?

"What have you done with Zandra?" I asked. "I know you're behind her disappearance, and you're responsible for what's happening to this town."

"Crimson Cove belongs to us, as does everyone who lives in it. We do with them as we will."

"Give me back Zandra!"

"What do we get in return?"

"Maybe I'll let you live. Maybe I won't. For what you've done to this town, you'll spend the rest of your lives behind bars. The angels will strip you of your magic."

There were several low chuckles. There were three of them. A trio.

"As if such a thing were even possible." This was a new voice. Another female. The last member of the trio.

I stamped a paw. "Show yourselves. I know you're hiding behind a kitten form. Who are you?"

There was a blur of movement, and the kittens appeared, looking as adorable as ever. But there was something different about them. It was exactly as Charlie described. Their forms shifted for a microsecond, so I wasn't certain what I saw. They blurred from tiny, adorable black kittens into large, looming, dark-robed shapes.

I sparked a spell in warning, but the kitten leading the trio shook her fluffy head. "Let's do nothing foolish. After all, you don't want everyone you love to die, do you?"

"Zandra's not dead. I feel our connection." I kept the spell alive, but they made no move to attack. "If you're here for me, don't punish her."

"That's exactly why we took her. We knew it would hurt you," the lead kitten said.

"You have Zandra?" My heart gave a painful thump.

"She was easy to scoop up. Without you by her side, it was barely a challenge."

I snarled at the trio. "This is all about me?"

"Isn't that what you tell everybody? The world revolves around the magnificent Juno. She needs to be the center of attention. It has been your undoing. Your arrogance has led to this moment."

"Your destruction of Crimson Cove has nothing to do with me," I said. "You did this. That was your choice."

"We didn't choose banishment and imprisonment, though," the lead kitten said.

"Is that something you think I did to you? I don't recall imprisoning three kittens. I can almost see through your disguise, so I know you're hiding from me. Who are you?"

"Age has poorly served you. You're forgetful. Anyone who meets us never forgets us."

I inhaled deeply and caught a whiff of pungent smoke. "That smoke. Your scent lingers..."

I stared hard at the kittens, trying to force my eyes to see the truth. There they were! Tall figures wearing cowled robes. My breath froze in my throat.

The trio chuckled as one, sensing my panic.

"Do you understand now why we're punishing you?" the lead kitten said, her form wavering and making me feel queasy.

"The only trio strong enough to take on a town as powerful as Crimson Cove were put away a long time ago," I said.

"Hmmm. Is that so? And does everyone who stays in prison remain there? Did you? We heard you escaped your most recent imprisonment."

Unease washed over me, and I unleashed a trickle of the power I'd absorbed. My vision shifted, and the kittens' forms blurred, turning them back into the cowled figures they'd been hiding. The scent of ancient burning wood swirled around me, so thick I almost choked on it.

My paws slid back as if my unconscious wanted me to flee. "It can't be!"

"Ah, joyous. You remember. We should send you a gift as a reward. Perhaps your witch's heart," the lead kitten said.

I growled a warning. "Stay away from Zandra. And you can't be here. It's not possible." Time felt like it slowed, and my vision tunneled on these creatures. The trio. Not kittens, but crones. Old as time. Deadly. Predators.

"And yet, here we are." The distorted image of the lead kitten danced on its paws, elongating and stretching.

"No! No one would ever be foolish enough to set you free," I said.

"Not by your hand. Or should I say paw?" the lead kitten—no, crone, said. "You wanted to ensure we'd never see the light of day again."

"I made sure there was no way out for you." I couldn't believe what I was seeing. I'd defeated the Crones of Blackened End. Hydra, Bashara, and Echo. They had tormented and harmed thousands before I'd finally stopped them.

"Times change, and people adapt. They become more tolerant. We were only ever doing what came naturally to us." Hydra, just like her sister crones, was concealed by a deep cowled robe, but I knew their faces. Long, thin, lined, with shimmering purple eyes, and fangs longer than a werewolf.

"Cursing a town's water supply to turn villagers into your mindless servants will never be approved of."

"Some townsfolk are stubborn."

"Creating a forest of flesh-eating trees from the remains of their enemies will always be a crime," I snarled. "Especially when you plant those trees in my domain."

The second crone, Bashara, shrugged. "What else should we do with the remains of our enemies?"

"Not murder them in the first place! And you brewed potions from stolen dreams to inflict insanity on those who tried to stop you."

Bashara cackled a laugh. "It's a pity that one didn't work on you."

"Juno hated it when we breached the veil between worlds, allowing dark entities passage to do our bidding," Hydra said. "That was one of my favorite hobbies."

"Just like you did with the Crypt witch prison," I said. "You broke the wards to get the demons out and make them your slaves."

"It was a simple task. The Crypt witches are too full of themselves. We showed them how weak and vulnerable they've become," Hydra said.

"My favorite pastime was wandering in our garden of poisonous plants, fertilized with the remains of that dwarf family who insulted us," Bashara said. "I always enjoyed taking cuttings to slip into the food and drink of deceivers who wronged us."

"It's unnatural to destroy villages and unleash darkness on innocent populations," I said. "That's why I had to stop you."

"You stopped us because you considered us a threat to your unpleasant rule. We saw fit to tease your subjects and show your vulnerabilities, and you despised us for that. We showed the world the magnificent Juno had flaws."

"I own up to my errors, but it's a rarity."

"There it is. Juno's over-inflated ego. We popped it, so you punished us," Hydra said.

"There are different kinds of magic," Bashara said. "It all has a place. Who are you to decide how we should use our powers?"

"Some magic should never be used. Yours corrupts and destroys. There is no purpose to that," I said.

"You considered us valuable when you had wars to win. You praised us and promoted us. Gave us a home. And then, when you were done with us, you decided we were more trouble than we were worth. Banished. Punished. Tossed aside. Cruel." Hydra hissed at me.

"That wasn't how it happened. Yes, you fought alongside me for many years. Then I heard the rumors of what you did when I left you unsupervised. Those rumors were all true. You had no right to take things. People. My people."

"It's called the spoils of war." Bashara inspected her long nails and bit the end off of one.

"Did I not pay you enough? Or praise you enough?" I still shuddered as I remembered the day I discovered their atrocities. It was risky, joining with the crones when facing a brutal enemy, but we'd made a deal. I was wrong to trust them.

And other things had distracted me. It was hard work, ruling over so many people. I lost focus, and the crones took advantage. When I learned the horrific truth, I'd acted immediately. The crones had been captured, tried, and imprisoned for the rest of their lives. Or so I thought.

"How did you get your powers back?" I asked.

"By doing what comes naturally," Hydra said. "We took from others. Just as we've been taking from the people of Crimson Cove. I see why you picked this town as your home. It's full of so much energy. And your ley lines are delicious."

"You're taking what isn't yours. And if you're draining power from the ley lines, that affects everyone."

"You have enough to share. You always were greedy, Juno," Bashara said.

"I'll admit to a few failings when I ruled. Things have changed," I said. "I don't want that anymore."

"Of course you do. Isn't that what this is all about?" Hydra sneered at me. "You long to get back everything taken from you by that sour-faced goblin."

"Which means you understand us," Bashara said. "You took everything we held dear and abandoned us. Now, we're reclaiming it."

"I have nothing in common with you," I spat. "Your magic is cruel and malevolent."

"Is it so different?" Hydra taunted. "Or has finding a good witch softened you? The Juno we knew would never have allowed us near her. A legion of guards would have surrounded her to keep her safe. And of course, her loyal subjects would have defended her until their last breath ran out."

"But you've made yourself vulnerable." Echo, the third crone, finally lifted her head. She'd always been the quiet one. The deadliest of the trio. "Which gave us the perfect opportunity to get our revenge."

"How did you even know I was here?"

"You kept your home a secret for a long time," Hydra said. "But rumor spreads, and enemies conspire."

"You still haven't told me how you escaped. The prison was impenetrable. I made sure of it."

"We took a leaf out of your book," Bashara said. "We turned into adorable kittens and slipped out. Or rather, we were carried out by a naive guard who took pity on three starving innocents."

"Someone must have helped you," I said. "I restrained your powers."

"You have more than a few enemies," Echo said with a smirk, flashing her fearsome fangs. "They found a way inside the prison. Gave us enough power to transform. Then, all we had to do was play the part. And now we take it all. We destroy you."

Rage burned through me. I flared a spell, furious at their deceit. Before I could hurl it, the crones combined their magic and wrapped it around me.

A thick, stifling heat engulfed me. The air reeked of burning power, and I was yanked from my paws, magic tearing through me.

I landed in the middle of Crimson Cove woods. The crones stood before me.

A row of bodies lay behind them.

Panic shot through me when I saw Zandra, Vorana, Sorcha, Sage, Sammy, Archie, Cythera, and a dozen other angels. I could barely breathe. I tugged on my bond with Zandra. It was so weak that I could barely feel it, but at least she was still with me. I could save her. I would save all of them.

"All dead!" Hydra said. "Because of you."

I longed to scream at them, to tell them I knew they were lying. But I kept my emotions locked down.

"Juno is so distraught, she can't speak," Bashara said, smirking.

"What a joy that is to see," Echo added.

"You deserve it," Hydra said. "There is no room for happiness in your life."

I stared at Zandra. Move. She had to move.

"You took everything from us," Echo said. "After we helped you."

"My sister crone feels things deeply. She has never forgiven you." Hydra rested a bony hand on Echo's shoulder.

"You broke our arrangement, Juno," Bashara said. "You must be punished."

Zandra's left pinky finger twitched. She was still fighting. Though everyone looked still and not even breathing, the crones hadn't killed them. They were suspended in magic.

"If you come quietly, I'll help you," I said. "You're right to be angry, but I had to serve you justice."

"You told us to win the battles for you, using whatever means necessary," Echo said. "That's what we did. And then you turned your back on us. You took everything and abandoned us."

"I had to. Your magic is malevolent."

"Oh, we're not so dissimilar. We all crave power. We all demand to be adored. Do you remember the pageants Juno would force her subjects to hold in her honor?" Hydra spun in a circle with her arms outstretched. "She expected frequent shows of loyalty."

"There was a time when I was like that," I admitted. "But then I met Zandra, and everything changed. I changed."

"Not enough," Bashara said. "You kept the most important things from those you claim to care about. Same old Juno."

"Your opinion means nothing to me," I said.

"It should," Hydra said. "You're the reason we're here. You are the reason the town you care about, and all the people you love, are in peril."

"We must punish her for what she did to us," Echo snapped.

"What will Juno do now?" Bashara taunted. "She has no bonded witch. No friends. Everyone has turned against her."

"She will find another witch," Echo sneered. "She uses people to get what she needs and then discards them. Sickening."

"I would never discard Zandra," I said fiercely. "I know what a true bond is."

"Is that bond worth dying for?" Hydra's tone forced a chill down my spine.

"Your anger doesn't give you the right to destroy everyone here," I said. "Confess to what you've done. I will speak up for you. I know your troubled history, so it'll be taken into account."

Hydra waved an arm, and a trail of dark gloopy magic dripped off her. "You have lost your edge. It took you too long to figure out we were tinkering with the Crypt witches."

"I'm still stunned you convinced the airhead angels that the word Tempest, the name of the most troublesome Crypt witch ever to walk this earth, written in the dirt under a corpse, wasn't involved in the murder," Echo said.

"We even ensured her magic was so muddled, she wasn't certain what day it was, let alone if she'd taken a life." Hydra lifted a shoulder. "Angel Force is an even bigger joke than Juno."

"It proved to us you still held great power over everyone," Bashara said. "Even in your diminished form."

"I'm glad the angels listen to me," I said. "You murdered Erick to drive a wedge between Zandra and Tempest. You wanted the Crypt witches in disarray."

"They're as wearisome as you are," Hydra said. "Why not destabilize that hateful power base? Those witches are smug and believe themselves to be unstoppable. Much like you."

"It was a condition of your freedom, wasn't it?" I asked. "A demon helped you escape my prison, provided you caused trouble for the Crypt witches.

You agreed because you learned of my connection to Zandra and planned to destroy two troublesome magical dynasties in one attack."

"It seemed like such a bargain." Hydra grinned, feral and sharp. "And your prison was less than perfect. It took little incentive to receive updates about you and gather our resources. And what do you know? In the flick of an enchanted wand, all the people you care about belong to us. Juno is not so loved, after all."

My hackles lifted. "You do not have control over my friends. Return them home."

"If you don't like what we're doing, try to stop us."

Power crackled between the crones, lifting their long hair and lighting their eyes with a sparkle of purple.

"It doesn't have to end this way," I said. "I remember when you fought for good. When you had justice in your hearts. Not cold, cruel vengeance. Give yourselves up."

"Oh no," Hydra hissed. "We will not come quietly, and we will not leave this town alone until it is nothing more than a smoldering ruin. A sad memory in your broken little heart."

"We intend to destroy you," Bashara added. "But first, we'll take away everyone you love in front of you. By the end, you'll be begging us to join them, because there'll be nothing left for you here."

The crones joined hands. A massive spiral of dark, flickering magic rolled out of them, a swirling maelstrom of power.

It was now or never. It was time to trust my old magic. The magic I'd hidden, dodged, and avoided for too long. I needed it to fight for everything I held dear.

Fight and win.

Because no one I loved was dying.

Chapter 19

Fight or die

The crones' dark magic surged toward me, a roiling storm of shadows and fire, thick with the scent of ancient smoky power and decay. I barely had time to throw up a shield before the first blast struck. My paws skidded against the earth as I braced myself, the force of it rattling through my bones.

"You're weaker than we expected, Juno," Hydra sneered. "All those years and time to perfect your magic, and this is all you have left?"

I didn't rise to the bait. I summoned my power, the deep, old magic that ran through my veins after so many decades of silence. It responded, curling around me like a living thing, eager for the fight.

I launched a counterattack, sending a torrent of silver fire streaking toward them. The crones moved in unison, their robes fluttering as they absorbed my magic. They were stronger together, feeding off one another's power like leeches.

Zandra lay motionless behind them, surrounded by our friends. I still felt our bond, but it was faint, like a dying ember. I had to end this fight before it was too late and I lost her forever.

"This town belongs to us, Juno. You should have fled when you had the chance," Bashara taunted. "It is your fault you're about to die."

I called on everything I had, weaving my magic into something raw and ancient. A storm of energy crackled around me. The crones shrieked as it lashed toward them, forcing them to retreat.

"Winning isn't an option for you," Echo hissed. "You don't even know what you are anymore. You're clinging to scraps of your past, while stuck in this mockery of servitude with a witch. You don't belong here. Nowhere is your home. Bleak, dark nothing. And we intend to send you there."

I kept a spell ready to toss. "I found my perfect witch. We belong here, and I intend to keep us together forever."

"All you've done is find a witch almost as broken as you are. That is the reason your bond is so strong. But you broke that bond with your lies. We know she no longer wants you."

Echo's words struck something deep in me, but I pushed it aside. "Maybe not. But I know one thing. You're not walking away from this. You've hurt my friends, family, and the town I adore. That is unforgivable."

The crones snarled, their forms shifting in and out of focus. Their kitten disguises had fully peeled away, leaving their true monstrous forms. They shimmered with an eerie glow. Their robes swirled with dark shifting magic, patterns of stars and stormy clouds flickering across the fabric. Raw energy crackled around them, occasionally sparking like distant lightning. And their eyes gleamed, promising nothing but pain.

They struck again, their combined magic a twisting, howling force of destruction. I dodged left, rolling as a jet of sickly green fire scorched the ground. I barely had time to counter before another attack slammed into my hastily thrown-up shield, sending me sprawling across the dirt. My ribs ached, but I forced myself up.

I flicked a paw, sending a shockwave through the ground. The earth split beneath them, jagged stone spears erupting skyward.

Bashara screeched as a rock caught the hem of her robe, pinning her in place. I twisted my magic again, sending chains snaking out to bind her, but before they could lock in place, Hydra countered, her spell slicing through my bindings like paper.

The battle raged on, magic clashing in a symphony of light and shadow. Every breath I took tasted of iron and smoke. I pushed harder, summoning storm winds to break through and reach Zandra, but the crones adapted, countering with punishing magic.

Shadows lengthened and thickened, forming clawed hands that reached for me, but I smashed them away and launched myself at the crones, claws crackling with power.

I struck Echo, my magic searing through her robes. She screamed, staggering back, but before

I could press the advantage, Hydra and Bashara retaliated.

A wall of magic slammed into me, lifting me off my paws and flinging me into a tree. Bark splintered under the impact, pain exploding through my body. I hit the ground, gasping.

The crones loomed closer, triumphant but then turned their attention away from me, their eyes narrowing on Zandra.

I felt it before I saw the energy shift, the gathering storm of their magic curling toward my friends like a spiked, poisoned vine intent on choking the life out of them.

"No!" I roared, throwing myself forward. A pulse of fire erupted from my murder mittens, slamming into Bashara. She hissed and recoiled, but the others pressed on, weaving spells too fast for me to counter.

A jagged bolt of dark magic shot toward Zandra. I flung out a shield, but it wasn't enough, and the spell impacted. Zandra jerked, pain flashing across her face. My heart slammed against my ribs as I raced toward her. I hurled a blast of energy, forcing the crones back long enough to crouch beside her.

"Stay with me," I whispered, my voice hoarse with fear. "I can beat them. I'd rather have you fighting by my side, but I can do this."

Zandra's eyes flickered as if she could hear me, but she grew limp as the magic worked through her.

A guttural growl made my blood run cold. But I had nothing to fear as Archie reared up and lunged at Bashara, his massive hellhound form blazing with fire. He sank his teeth into the swirling magic of her robes, dragging her back. But Bashara twisted her fingers, a tendril of shadow wrapping around his throat.

Archie yelped, his fire flickering as he thrashed, fighting the suffocating grip of her magic.

"No, no, no!" I launched myself at him, slicing through the shadowy bonds with a desperate spell. He crumpled to the ground, panting, his usually bright eyes dimmed with pain.

"You can't save them all, Juno," Echo sneered. "Your power is stretched too thin. Choose who lives and who dies. Perhaps we should punish the hellhound for fighting our magic."

"He's a strong one. We should recruit him," Bashara said.

"The beast must die for his disrespect." Hydra swept a hand over my fallen friends. "They must all perish."

I refused to believe that would happen. My chest heaved as my magic surged, wild and raw, pushing past the exhaustion. I had no time for doubt that this power would ensure I won this fight.

I planted myself between my friends and the crones, deflecting every spell they hurled, dodging attacks, hexes, and curses. I was fighting to protect my family.

The crones lashed out again, their magic twisting toward Zandra's fallen form.

I planted my paws and summoned a barrier just in time. The spell slammed into my shield, sending a sharp jolt of agony through me. I held firm. I had to.

Through the haze of magic, Zandra stirred, her fingers twitching. Hope flared inside me. She was fighting as hard as I was.

"I'm not letting you take them," I growled at the crones, fire sparking along my fur.

They hesitated for the first time, their swirling forms flickering like candle flames in a storm.

A hissed whisper spread between them, and their eyes glowed. They linked hands and pointed at Zandra.

They would not kill my wonderful witch.

Gritting my teeth, I gathered my strength once more. The last of the magic stones. The ones I carried, the ones I'd hoarded, too afraid to reclaim my power for fear everything would change. They had immense power, and it was time to use it. I had to relinquish my hope of regaining everything taken from me when I became an enchanted cat.

A deep sadness settled over me, but it was brief. The choice was simple.

I flipped off the collar, dropped the stones into the dirt, and stepped on them. They pulsed, resisting for a second as if they knew what I intended to do. But I was stronger. This wasn't about me anymore. I could will my magic to do anything.

With a guttural growl, I slammed them into the ground. The explosion of energy ripped through the clearing, sending shockwaves in every direction. The crones staggered back, screaming as the magic they'd been siphoning from this town was redirected.

But not into me. It went into Zandra and my friends. Where it belonged.

The magic filled them, spiraling out of the crones as if grateful for a release from imprisonment in such bitter, broken bodies.

But it wasn't enough. No one was opening their eyes. My friends were too weak.

They needed more power. They needed my magic.

I hesitated. Demi-goddess power was all-consuming, but spread among so many, it may be diluted enough for them to handle. They'd never be the same, but better changed and magically different—magical misfits—than dead.

I pressed a paw to my head and unleashed the stones' magic into my friends, calling it to leave me and save them.

A bright, fierce light flaring around them dazzled me.

Zandra gasped as she jerked upright, her eyes flying open. Our bond snapped into place, stronger than before. The others stirred, color returning to their faces as my magic restored them.

The crones screamed as the power turned against them. Their illusions shattered, their true, withered forms exposed to the world. No longer terrifying figures cloaked in darkness, they were just ancient, bitter creatures, shriveled and powerless now that their leech-like draining had stopped.

Exhaustion hit me like a tidal wave, but I forced myself to stay standing. I'd done it.

The crones had lost.

Before I could catch my breath and check on Zandra, a sharp, electric charge crackled through the clearing, and a huge troop of angels appeared.

Cythera landed first, her wings unfurled in a display of barely restrained fury. The air shimmered with an intensity that could melt steel, her piercing blue eyes burning like twin stars. Uh oh. She was angry.

"Juno," she snapped, voice like a whip crack. "What have you done?"

"Greetings, Cythera." I straightened, ignoring the ache in every part of my body. "I stopped the Blackened End crones. You may have heard of them. Or not. They were to spend the rest of their days in prison. Sadly, that plan failed. I'm Plan B. Aren't you pleased I broke out of your cell now?"

Cythera's gaze flicked to the crones, now collapsed and barely conscious as their stolen magic slowly leaked out of them, then returned to me. "You stopped them? Or did your presence bring them here?"

"Semantics. Maybe they are here because of me, but I didn't summon them. And I had nothing to do with their escape. Untrustworthy guards and a sneaky demon are behind this. I must find out who and punish them."

Cythera stepped forward, her wings twitching. "They have wreaked havoc because of you."

"I see you still have some anger issues to work through." I shuffled closer to Zandra, who was wobbling to her feet. "Take deep breaths while I check on everyone."

"My anger issues are all your fault!" Cythera lowered her wings. "But... I will admit to suddenly feeling less murderous."

"Now I've stopped the crones, everyone will return to their usual selves." I flicked a glance at my friends. "Well, almost. I'll greatly appreciate your heartfelt and continuous thanks."

Cythera snarled at me but raised a hand in apology.

"Hey! Enough snapping and growling. Juno saved us all." Zandra shuffled over to join me, confusion on her face and a new magical light glowing in her eyes. "I'm not sure what she did, but I was dying. Frozen, numb, and scared witless. My magic was gone."

"It was simple enough." I rested a paw on Zandra's knee, and she nodded to let me know I could leap onto her shoulder. "I gave you my magic. You all have some. It was the only way to free you from the crones' icy clutches. They leech magic and joy. They took what didn't belong to them and used it against you."

Zandra glanced at me. "That's what I'm feeling? Your magic?"

"We'll talk later. You may need to practice. My magic differs from witch magic."

Cythera didn't even look at Zandra or anyone else as they slowly got to their feet and paws. Her focus was solely on me. "The higher courts will decide what to do with you, Juno. You've long walked a fine line, but not anymore. This is out of my hands."

"There's no need for a trial. I'll make the higher angels see sense," I said. "I'll contact Tinkerbell. She'll put in a good word for me."

"There won't be time to do that. They're already here." Cythera stepped back and lowered her head.

An older male with golden wings and a look of mild disinterest on his ridiculously handsome face appeared beside her, adjusting the scarf draped around his shoulders.

"Who are you?" I leaned against Zandra's head. I recognized him as a higher angel, but we were strangers.

"The decider of your fate, sweetie." He swept into a bow.

"And we know all about you." Another higher angel, a younger man with soft, feathered wings that seemed ruffled, sighed. "Why is it always Juno causing drama? I had plans today! Good ones. A lovely little mortal bakery with the most divine pastries, and now I'm dealing with this because the others were too busy."

"And we were already here to do that dull little efficiency audit."

"Oh, yes. We'll have to start that again. The fire destroyed the paperwork. Or was it Cythera? Her temper has been legendary. That'll go in the report. Anger management training for you, my sweet."

"I have not been myself," Cythera muttered.

"Such drama in such a small place." The older angel sighed. "We shall have to make alterations. Change is afoot. And who enjoys that? But endure it, we must."

"I don't cause drama," I said. "I help. Tell them, Cythera."

Cythera shook her head. "The higher angels have been watching you. Your power makes them nervous. They'll be reviewing this incident with a critical eye."

"Make that a disapproving eye," the younger angel chimed in. "Do you know how hard it is to enjoy a perfectly crafted pastry when one is yanked into yet another Juno-related disaster?"

"I've never pulled you into one of my disasters!"

"And what's the obsession with pastries?" Zandra asked. "Cythera, you can't leave Juno's fate in their hands. They have no clue what they're talking about."

"They were here conducting the branch efficiency review when everything went wrong." Cythera looked a touch apologetic. "The order came down to investigate. The task fell to them because they were closest."

"But not the most qualified," Zandra snapped.

Cythera pinched the bridge of her nose. She turned sharply, fixing her gaze on the crones. "I want them bound in the strongest containment magic we have."

The older angel huffed a breath and waved Cythera's angel troop back. "We'll do that. We can't afford any more errors, can we? No more escaping magical cats. Or ley lines being naughty. Crimson Cove is stirring interest among the highers, my sweet, and for the wrong reasons."

"Ugh, containment duty," his companion grumbled. "I didn't come here to shackle a bunch of grumpy old witches. I feel lied to. I'm sure this type of work isn't in my contract."

"Those grumpy old witches used to flatten towns by clicking their bony fingers, so be careful not to underestimate them," I said.

The younger angel peered at the crones. "They look like they're struggling to breathe."

"Don't say I didn't warn you."

The higher angels groused and discussed pastries as they weaved intricate chains of glowing light around the crones. The magic crackled, sealing into place with a resounding snap. These angels may not know what they were talking about when it came to my successes, but they were powerful.

Cythera's gaze swept over the clearing before landing back on me. "Juno, you're coming with us. We need information before the higher angels make a decision."

I bristled. "A decision about what? I saved this town and everyone in it, including you, and you want to drag me in like a criminal?"

"Whenever you're involved in an investigation, it always gets complicated. Bringing the Blackened End crones to Crimson Cove is about as complicated as it gets. We need information."

"There's no point in arguing," Zandra muttered to me. "We'll sort this when Cythera is calmer and the higher angels have gone off pastry hunting instead of meddling in our business."

She was right, but I was wary of what Cythera meant about a decision. They had to come to their senses and know I wasn't to blame. I was the epic heroine in this adventure.

As the angels finished their work, a gentle hand slipped into my fur. Zandra. My wonderful witch was back with me. She watched me with quiet concern.

"Are you okay?" she murmured.

I exhaled slowly. "I will be now I have you back. We are together, aren't we? Still bonded? I know we have matters to unpick."

"I reckon we do, but we're good. The crones' magic messed with me, too. I'd never abandon you. I said things I didn't mean."

I glanced at the blackened patch of dirt where I'd unleashed my magic. The stones were gone, their power spent and channeled into those I loved the most. My old magic had truly left me.

And strangely, I was fine with that. Because Zandra was alive, and so were my friends. Crimson Cove was safe and the crones defeated.

But from the look in Cythera's eyes, I was anything but safe. And without my magic, I wasn't sure I could beat her.

Chapter 20

The end

The next evening, I sat in Vorana's yard, paws curled under me, eyes gritty from lack of sleep. After being questioned for hours by Angel Force, I'd been allowed home. I'd stayed up talking through everything with Zandra and my friends. They now knew what kind of power they had in them, but it would take time to adjust.

Zandra paced in front of me, crackling with my magic. She'd buzzed with energy all day, and I didn't blame her. She had power now. Real, untamed, dangerous power. And it was my job to ensure she didn't burn down the town by accident. My wonderful witch was used to Crypt witch magic, but this was on a whole other level.

"I don't understand why I can't get it to do what I want," she huffed, shoving her sleeves up. "I think about the spell, I focus, but then—" She flicked her fingers, and a blast of purple light shot out, narrowly missing a stone garden hare looking at the sky and slamming into a tree. The trunk groaned as frost spread over the bark. "That happens."

"You're forcing it," I said. "My magic is about balance. You can't just shove it in one direction and expect it to behave."

Zandra made a frustrated noise, running a hand through her hair. "That's easy for you to say. You've had this magic forever. Exactly how old are you again?"

"Old enough not to answer that question." *Had.* The word stung, but I ignored it. I'd made my choice. And I'd make it again. "Try once more. But this time, don't push it. Guide it."

Zandra took a deep breath, closed her eyes, and lifted her hands. Magic coiled around her fingers like mist. For a moment, it held, shimmering softly, and I thought she had it. Then it surged forward, spiraling toward the ground, and a blast of wind sent dirt and leaves flying.

"This is impossible," she muttered. "Maybe I'm not meant to have your power. It doesn't work with mine. Why not take it back?"

"I don't know how. Once gifted, it can't be restored." I sighed. "You can handle any power. You need practice. Let's try something smaller. Call the magic, but don't use your hands. Just let it settle."

She frowned but nodded, closing her eyes again. This time, the power came slower. Softer. The air shimmered. No wild explosions. No ice bolts. Just magic, humming around her like an old friend.

"Good," I said. "Now open your eyes. Keep the feeling. Don't rush it. My magic is bound to feelings and thoughts."

"I don't like the sound of that. You know I have a temper." Zandra's gaze locked on mine. For the first time all day, she wasn't forcing it. She was just... being.

A flicker of something stirred in my chest. Pride, maybe. Or regret. If I'd held onto my magic, I'd be right there with her, feeling the rush, the connection. But I'd made my choice. And looking at Zandra, steady and glowing with potential, I knew I'd done the right thing.

"You're getting it."

Zandra let out a breathless laugh. "Kind of. Let's try something more advanced. Something you would've done."

I narrowed my eyes. "Like what?"

She didn't answer. Instead, she raised both hands, calling the energy differently this time. Not wild and erratic, but focused, precise. A shimmering portal flickered into existence a few feet away. It wavered, unstable, but then snapped into clarity, revealing a distant landscape through its swirling edges.

I blinked. "That's not basic magic."

She grinned. "I want to see if I can handle it. Ancient goddess power."

The portal pulsed as she adjusted her stance, her fingers twitching as she tried to keep it open. It held for another few seconds before suddenly contracting then bursting apart with a pop of displaced air. The force knocked her back a step.

Zandra groaned. "Ugh. I almost had it."

I padded closer, scanning her carefully. "You're pushing hard, but you're getting there. You need to learn when to let go before the magic fights back."

"Are you two still at it?" Vorana came out of the house. Her hair sparked with energy, tiny embers flickering at the ends. She carried a large plate of perfect-looking brownies.

Sage, her sleek fur bristling with stray sparks, scowled as she stomped beside Vorana. "I keep bursting into flames! I've not been allowed in my papoose in case I set fire to Vorana." Her tail singed the grass before she huffed and stomped it out.

Zandra rubbed her forehead as though she had the headache of a century. "We're figuring things out. Crimson Cove will be different now. Juno's magic is everywhere. We'll all have to adapt."

"At least the house appliances are working again. Although these fiery sparks that keep flying out of me will take getting used to." Vorana nodded, glancing around. The air was faintly tinged with gold and deep indigo, the remnants of my ancient magic lingering.

I'd changed the town in a way I never imagined, twisting through its foundations, its buildings, and its people. "The sparks will fade. It's just the magic settling in."

Vorana offered the brownies. "Nothing will be the same. But a change is as good as a rest."

"I always go for the rest option." Sage huffed, flicking her ear in irritation. "We don't need more unpredictability."

Vorana chuckled, the embers in her hair flaring. "Come inside. We need to demolish these brownies. And I've got a pot roast in the oven."

As we settled at the worn wooden table in the kitchen, the soft hum of magic vibrated through the air. The house walls breathed with enchantment, my magic seeping into every crevice. It was intoxicating, unpredictable, and overwhelming all at once. I'd forgotten just how powerful I'd been.

Sage nudged her food bowl, and a flicker of energy crackled over her paw and pinged her head. She groaned, ears flattening. "This is my life now."

"But you have a life, thanks to Juno." Vorana kissed the top of Sage's head. "We all have."

"And new magic doesn't settle overnight," I said.

"It's old magic. Super old," Sage said.

"It's new to me." Vorana held out her hands, laughing as magic shimmered across her skin. "After feeling so sick and tired, I'm happy. Although we'll need new rules for the town. I heard from Sorcha that people are having... incidents. Tia and Binky's bakery door turned into a portal and tried to suck several passersby inside! And there's a group of garden gnomes roaming around, looking confused."

"I have the zoomies again! I need space to run." Sage jumped off her chair and bounded out the back door.

We followed her to the door, Vorana and Zandra munching on brownies.

"We'll get back to normal." Zandra lifted me onto her shoulder. "The town just needs time to try on its new magic."

"My world won't have magic," I said. "I'm not sure how long that will take to adjust to."

"You got a spark earlier," Zandra said. "It could come back. You need time, too."

I had felt a faint flicker of something when casting a spell, but I couldn't sense what it was. I felt like a new witch with no knowledge and little talent.

"You'll have to do things the old-fashioned way, with whispered spells and brewing potions," Vorana said.

I wrinkled my booping snooter. That sounded like hard work.

Vorana laughed as Sage raced around the yard, not slowed by her harness. In fact, her back legs were twitching. Perhaps my magic gift meant she could leave behind her harness for good.

I leaned against Zandra's head, happy to be reconciled with my now insanely powerful witch. "If you want to look for a familiar with power, I'll understand."

She gave me a look from the side of her eye. "What do you mean?"

"I've always been the one in charge. Now, our roles are reversed. I'm your sidekick, and you need a sidekick who can watch your back."

Zandra smirked and shook her head. "I know I've always been your second fiddle, but just because things have shifted, I still want you. And like Vorana said, we just need to adjust. It might even be fun, me being in charge."

Her mobile snow globe buzzed, and she pulled it from her pocket.

I saw Tempest's face. Wiggles squished in beside her. As soon as we'd gotten back on our feet and paws, we'd checked in with the residents of Willow Tree Falls. Life was returning to normal there now the crones had been stopped.

"I should take this." Zandra grinned. "And we need to plan a visit home where we can chill and not do battle with demons."

The air above us cracked like a whip, and Finn shot down from the sky, his wings flaring as he landed in the yard. His chest heaved, his face pale.

"Juno, run!" he gasped, eyes wild.

I stiffened. "What's going on?"

Finn glanced at the sky then back at me, his panic palpable. "The higher angels have made their decision. Cythera's coming for you. You're being charged with attempting to destroy Crimson Cove!"

The world tilted. "That's ridiculous. I saved this town."

Finn shook his head. "The higher angels consider you dangerous. They want to strip you of everything. Your power, your freedom."

My stomach dropped. "For life?"

Finn nodded grimly. "For life. You have to go. Now."

Zandra clutched me tight against her head. "Juno stopped the crones. She protected all of us."

Finn's wings twitched with urgency. "The higher angels see it differently. They think your magic is unpredictable. Letting you roam free is a risk they won't take anymore."

"They can't listen to the two higher angels who were sniping and complaining about pastries!" Zandra said. "We want a second opinion."

Finn shook his head. "It's not just them. The angels have been watching Juno. They knew about her demi-goddess power. Now she's released it, they don't trust her."

"Into the whole town! We all have some of that power," Zandra said. "Are they planning on banishing all of us?"

Finn gulped. "Just Juno."

A deep chill spread through me. This wasn't just a warning. This was a sentence. If the higher angels got their way, I'd never see Crimson Cove again. They'd separate me from Zandra and everyone I loved.

A distant hum filled the air. Magic, strong and pressing, approached fast. It had a faint sugary scent. Which meant only one thing.

"Juno, we don't have time," Finn said. "Go!"

The ground trembled, and shadows stretched unnaturally. I swallowed hard, knowing what was at stake. I had a choice. Fight or flee. But either way, my life in Crimson Cove was over.

The air split with a deafening crack as Cythera appeared, her wings unfurling in a blaze of light. And she wasn't alone. The force of the angels' arrival sent ripples of power through the ground, making the grass tremble.

"Juno, I am arresting you for crimes against magical stability," Cythera announced.

I jumped down from Zandra's shoulder, ears pinned back. "That's absurd."

Cythera's eyes locked onto mine. "Your reckless use of magic has compromised the balance. You are a threat, and threats must be neutralized."

Finn hovered nearby, shifting uneasily. "Cythera, maybe we should—"

Her gaze snapped to him, silencing his protest. "This is not up for debate. The higher angels have passed judgment."

"And they always get things right?" I flicked a glance at the two pastry-obsessed higher angels who stood close by. One of them had a paper bag in hand, no doubt full of delicious snacks from Tia's bakery. How could their decision be trusted?

Zandra moved beside me, her hands clenched. "Juno did nothing wrong. I would be dead if it wasn't for her."

Cythera ignored Zandra. "Juno, surrender your remaining magic. Now."

"What magic? I gave it away to keep the people I love and the town I call home safe. You're making a mistake."

A hush settled over the yard, a silence that signaled a moment before the chaos.

Cythera pulled out a crystal etched with glowing marks. Finn shifted behind her, his feathers ruffling with unease.

Zandra's breathing was heavy beside me. "We can still run," she whispered.

"We don't run," I murmured back. "We stand. I'm innocent."

"Will you come quietly?" Cythera asked.

I shook my head.

Cythera raised her hand, magic lashing toward me like a bolt of golden lightning. The blast struck the ground, leaving a scorched mark on Vorana's carefully tended yard.

"That was a warning," Cythera said, her voice icy. "Stop resisting and accept your fate."

"My fate isn't to spend the rest of my days devoid of magic and without my family. You've made the wrong decision. Come back when logic has prevailed."

"It is a decision I must stick to." A flicker of something, maybe regret, crossed Cythera's face before she steadied herself and determined resolution settled in place.

I braced myself. "Then take your best shot."

"Very well." She lifted both hands, radiating raw celestial energy.

Before Cythera could strike, Zandra lunged. She didn't throw magic wildly like before. This time, she reached for the magic in the air, weaving a protective shield between me and Cythera. The force of Cythera's attack slammed against it, sending sparks flying.

"You'll have to go through me," Zandra growled, standing her ground. "We belong together. You won't split us up."

Cythera's wings flared. A second blast of energy roared toward us.

I had to fight back, but with what? My magic was gone. I had nothing left but words. "This isn't justice. This is fear talking. I'm not a threat."

Zandra threw another wave of magic at Cythera. Her celestial energy swallowed it, rendering it useless. Cythera sent Zandra sprawling to the ground.

I rushed to her side, but before I could help her, chains of light snapped around me, tightening instantly. A burning sensation shot through me as

Cythera's magic took hold. I struggled, but there was no breaking free.

"It's over," Cythera said. "The higher angels have ruled. You are to be exiled to Badger's Haze."

The words hit harder than any magic ever could. Badger's Haze! A desolate place, devoid of all hope, and riddled with negative despair. My heart pounded. I'd fought so hard, sacrificed so much... and now I was being cast away like a villain.

Zandra pushed herself up. "No! You can't do this. We're bonded."

"The decision is final," Cythera said.

"Change your minds," I yelled at the higher angels. "Let me plead my case."

They shrugged in unison. One of them finger waved at me. To them, I was nothing.

The golden chains tightened, and with a swipe of her hand, Cythera cast the unalterable part of my sentence. The world dissolved into blinding light.

Zandra cursed, eyes blazing with defiance as she threw out spell after spell.

Cythera spread her wings as she knocked away the spells, the glow around her intensifying. "Your exile begins now."

I exhaled slowly, forcing my voice to remain steady despite this devastating outcome. "Shame on you. Why didn't you stand up for me? We're friends. Friends help each other."

The expression of regret appeared again before fading as the light swallowed me whole.

I glimpsed Zandra's panicked face just as a rush of cold hit me, the weight of the spell pressing down on me like an invisible cage. My stomach lurched as the world twisted, yanking me through space, through something that felt like tearing and reassembling all at once. I tried to brace myself, but I was weightless, powerless.

Then, the ground slammed into me.

I hit hard, rolling through damp earth and dead leaves. My paws trembled as I forced myself to stand, my vision swimming.

The air here was thick, heavy with moisture and the scent of rot. Gnarled trees loomed around me, their twisted branches blocking out the sky. A low mist clung to the ground, shifting like it was alive.

Badger's Haze. My prison.

I flicked my tail, trying to steady myself. I was alone. No Zandra, no Sammy, no allies. Just me, surrounded by the eerie quiet of this forsaken place.

A rustling caught my ear. I turned sharply, my muscles tensed. I had no magic, no defenses, but I wasn't about to cower.

Whatever was out there, watching me from the shadows, would soon learn that, exile or not, I wasn't beaten yet.

And I would get home and back to Zandra. One day.

Juno will return in the spinoff series **The Feline Files.**

Also by

Witch Haven: Welcome to Witch Haven, where nothing is what it seems. Meet four fabulous witches as they struggle with their destinies, deal with misfiring magic, murder, and the Magic Council.

Crypt Witches: Meet Tempest Crypt, a witch who swallows demons, and Wiggles, her mini talking hellhound, while you enjoy magical murder and intrigue.

Lorna Shadow: A cozy mystery series set in the fun world of a personal assistant who sees ghosts. Meet Lorna, her ditzy sidekick, Helen, and Flipper, the dog who senses ghosts, as they solve crimes and save the day.

Holly Holmes: An adorable cozy culinary mystery series set in the beautiful village of Audley St. Mary. Each book is full of treats, murder, and twists. Join Holly and Meatball, her clue-hunting dog, as they solve murders and eat cake.

About the author

K.E. O'Connor (Karen) is a cozy mystery author living in the beautiful British countryside. She loves all things mystery, animals, and cake.

When she's not writing, she volunteers at a local animal sanctuary, reads a ton of books, binge watches mystery series, and dreams of living somewhere warmer.

To stay in touch with the mysteries, where the killer always gets caught, justice is served magic style, and the familiars talk, join her newsletter.

Newsletter:
www.subscribepage.com/cozymysteries
Website: www.keoconnor.com
Facebook: www.facebook.com/keoconnorauthor

www.ingramcontent.com/pod-product-compliance
Lightning Source LLC
Chambersburg PA
CBHW050610190726
48283CB00007B/2362